EACH GOOD VS EVIL BOOK HAS TWO STORIES —
ONE BLUE AND ONE RED — BUT YOU CAN READ
IT MANY DIFFERENT WAYS . . .

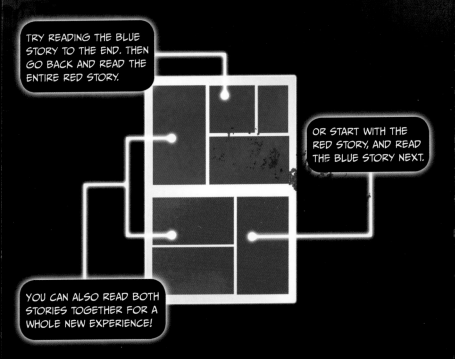

TRY READING THE BLUE
STORY TO THE END. THEN
GO BACK AND READ THE
ENTIRE RED STORY.

OR START WITH THE
RED STORY, AND READ
THE BLUE STORY NEXT.

YOU CAN ALSO READ BOTH
STORIES TOGETHER FOR A
WHOLE NEW EXPERIENCE!

# IT'S UP TO YOU!

READ THIS BOOK AGAIN AND AGAIN TO DISCOVER EXCITING,
NEW DETAILS IN THE NEVER-ENDING BATTLE OF . . . GOOD VS EVIL.

# Dungeon of Seven Dooms

by
Michael Dahl

illustrated by
Roberta Pares

STONE ARCH BOOKS
a capstone imprint

Story by Michael Dahl
Illustrated by Roberta Pares
Color by Glass House Graphics
Series Designer: Brann Garvey
Series Editor: Donald Lemke
Editorial Director: Michael Dahl
Art Director: Bob Lentz
Creative Director: Heather Kindseth

WWW.CAPSTONEPUB.COM

Good vs Evil is published by Stone Arch Books,
151 Good Counsel Drive, P.O. Box 669, Mankato, Minnesota 56002
Copyright © 2012 by Stone Arch Books.

Library of Congress Cataloging-in-Publication Data
Dahl, Michael.
   Dungeon of Seven Dooms / written by Michael Dahl ; illustrated by
Glass House Graphics.
      p. cm. -- (Good vs. evil)
   ISBN 978-1-4342-2091-2 (library binding)
1.  Graphic novels. [1. Graphic novels. 2. Princes--Fiction. 3.
Monsters--Fiction. 4. Good and evil--Fiction.]  I. Glass House
Graphics. II. Title.
   PZ7.7.D34Du 2010
   741.5'973--dc22
2010004117

Summary: Young Prince Arel has been imprisoned by his evil brother,
Prince Kalban, who seeks to steal the throne. Arel must use his wits and
his sword arm to battle through the monstrous traps of the Dungeon of
the Seven Dooms in order to rescue his father and save the kingdom.

PRINTED IN THE UNITED STATES OF AMERICA IN STEVENS POINT, WISCONSIN.
032011    006111WZF11

"WHAT DUNGEON IS SO DARK AS ONE'S OWN HEART?"
—NATHANIEL HAWTHORNE

# PRINCE KALBAN

IN AN ANCIENT KINGDOM OF LIGHT AND SHADOW, ON THE NIGHT OF THE DRAGON'S STAR, PRINCE KALBAN IMPRISONS HIS TWIN BROTHER, THE RIGHTFUL HEIR TO THE THRONE. THEN KALBAN AND HIS HENCHMEN BEGIN THEIR MARCH THROUGH THE HEAVILY GUARDED PALACE, TO ATTACK THE KING, AND CROWN THE EVIL KALBAN AS THE NEXT RULER . . .

# GOOD vs EVIL

# PRINCE AREL

ON THE NIGHT OF THE DRAGON'S STAR, AREL IS IMPRISONED BY HIS EVIL TWIN BROTHER IN THE DUNGEON OF SEVEN DOOMS. NO ONE HAS EVER ESCAPED FROM THE WEIRD PRISON. BUT AREL MUST FIND A WAY THROUGH THE MAZE OF DEATH AND SHADOW, TO DEFEAT HIS BROTHER, AND RESCUE THE KINGDOM'S RIGHTFUL RULER . . .

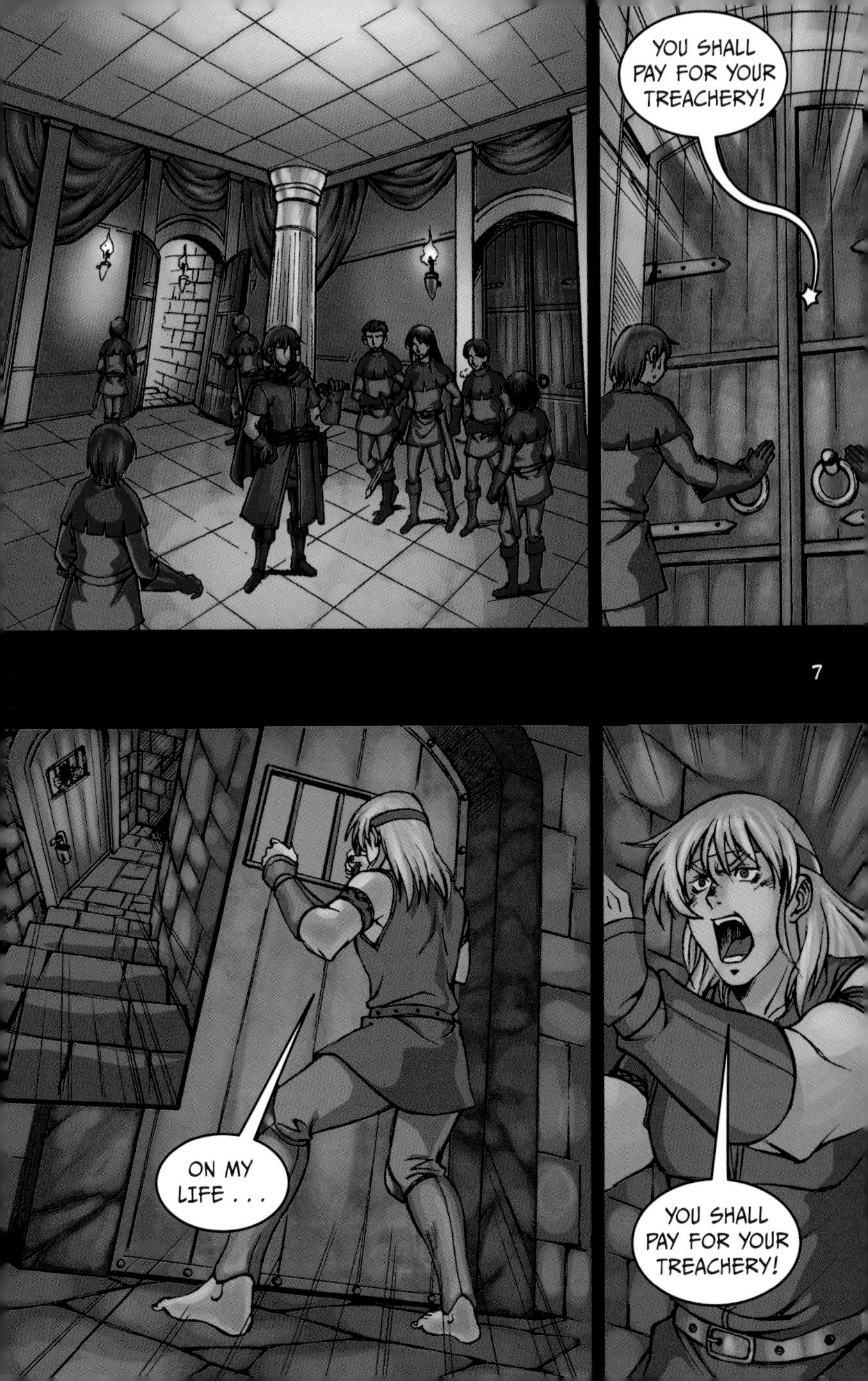
YOU SHALL PAY FOR YOUR TREACHERY!
ON MY LIFE . . .
YOU SHALL PAY FOR YOUR TREACHERY!

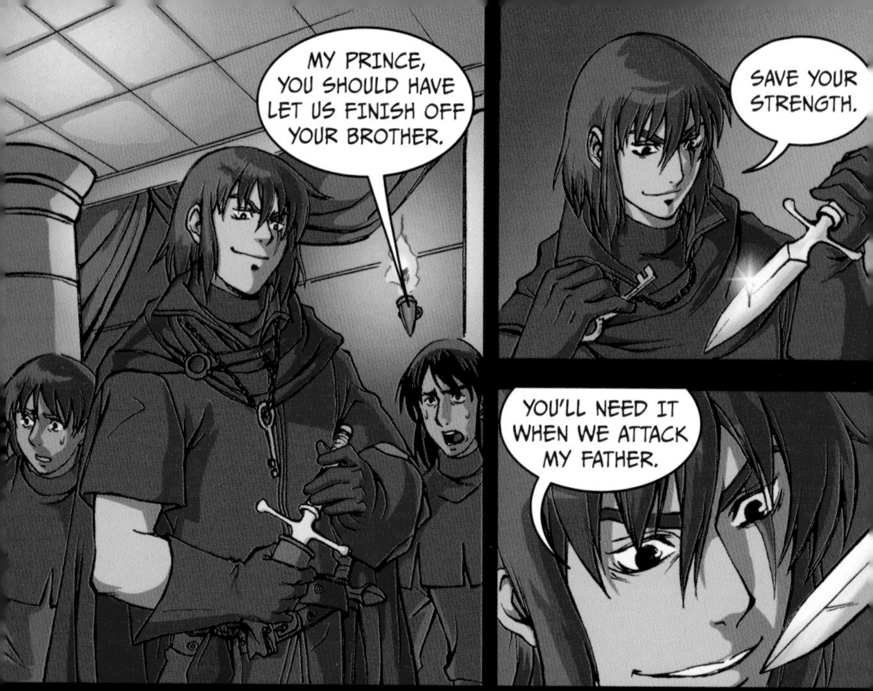
MY PRINCE, YOU SHOULD HAVE LET US FINISH OFF YOUR BROTHER.
SAVE YOUR STRENGTH.
YOU'LL NEED IT WHEN WE ATTACK MY FATHER.



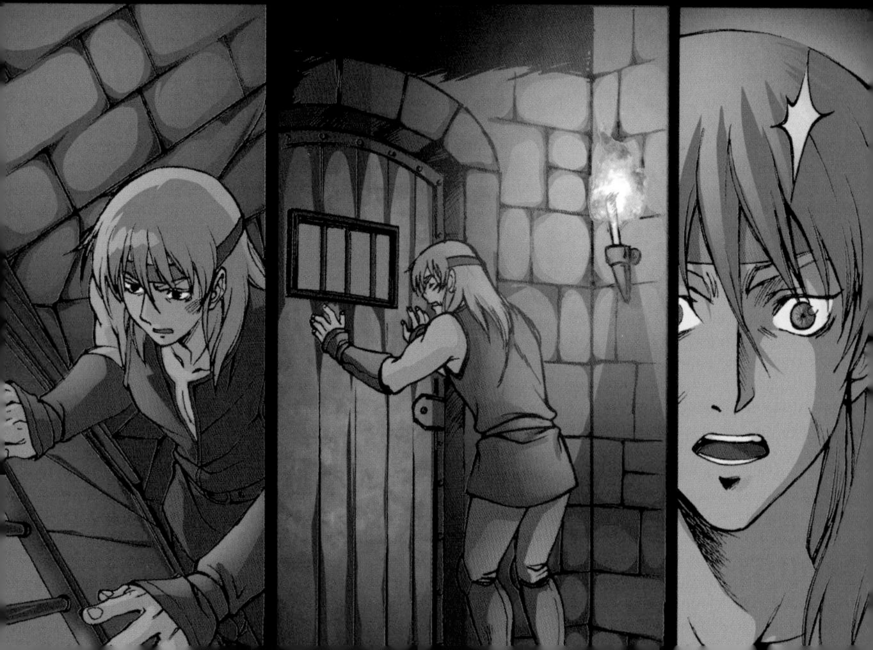

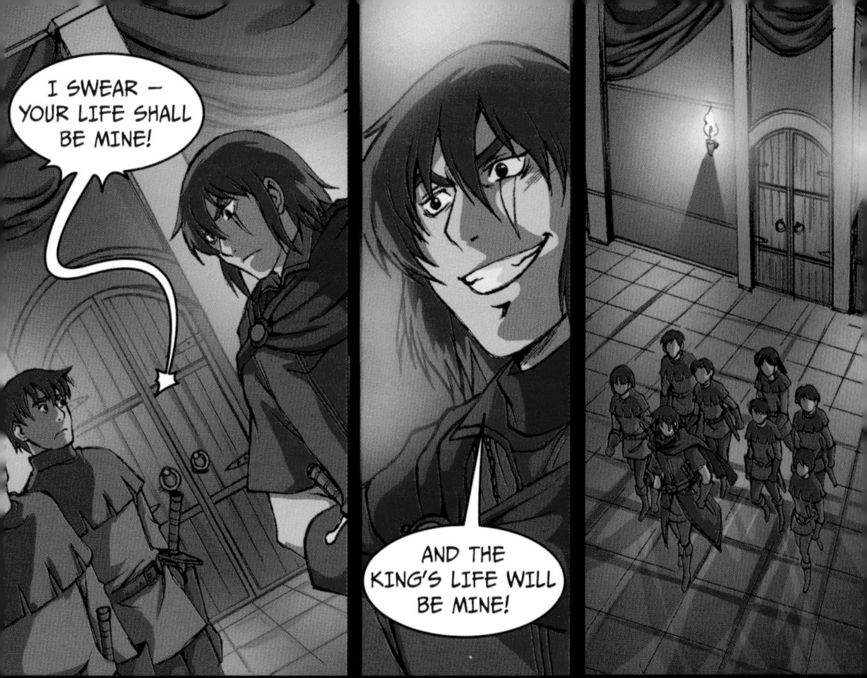
I SWEAR — YOUR LIFE SHALL BE MINE!
AND THE KING'S LIFE WILL BE MINE!



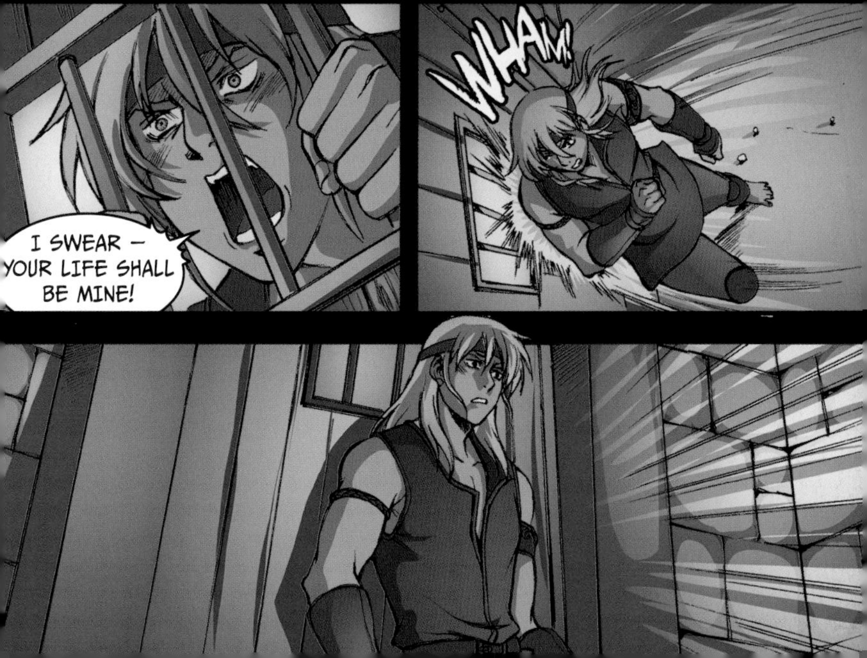
I SWEAR — YOUR LIFE SHALL BE MINE!
WHAM!

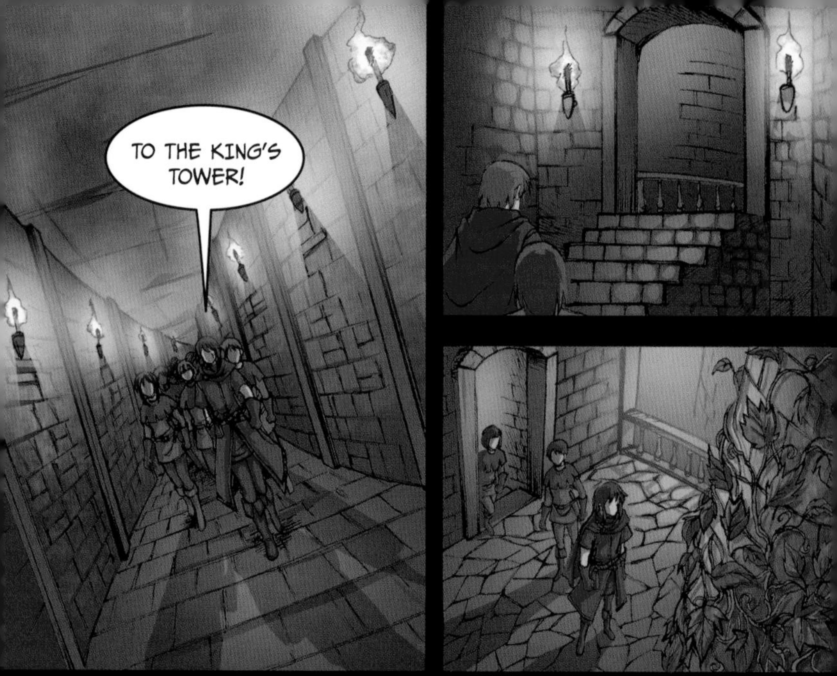
TO THE KING'S TOWER!



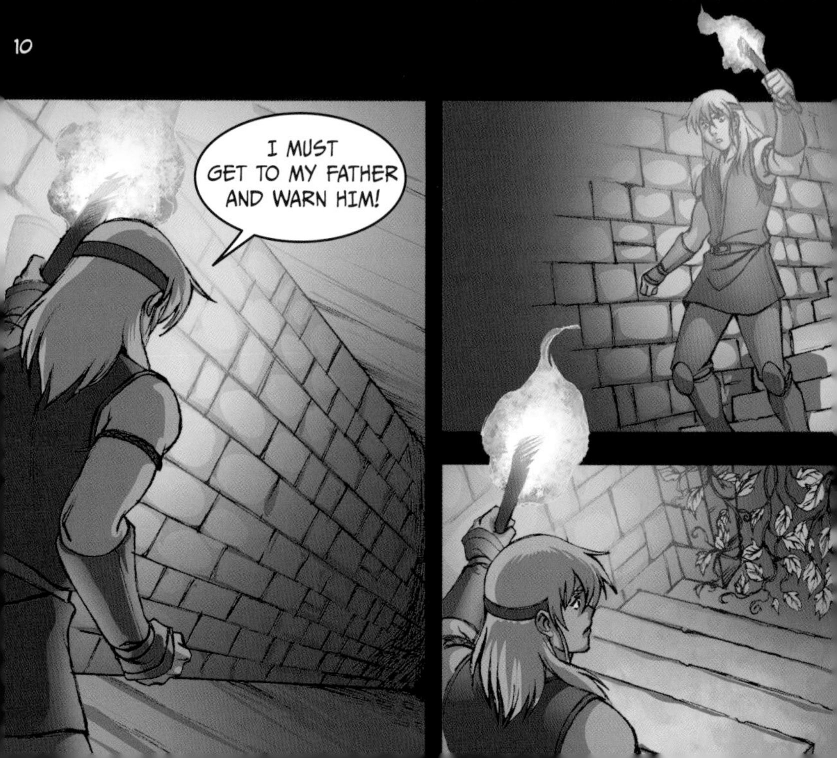
I MUST GET TO MY FATHER AND WARN HIM!

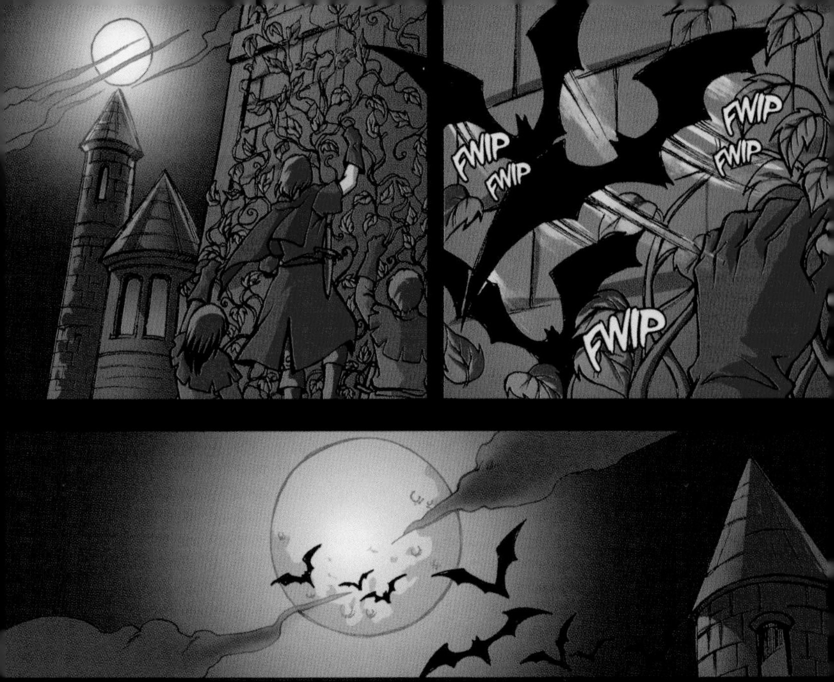
FWIP
FWIP
FWIP
FWIP
FWIP



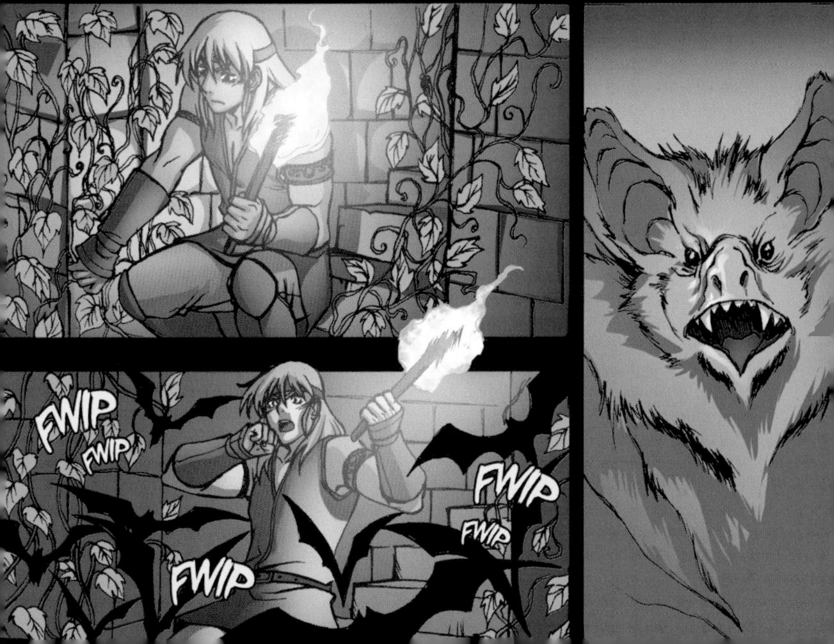
FWIP
FWIP
FWIP
FWIP
FWIP

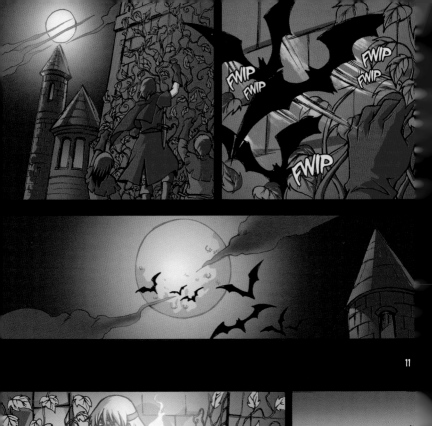

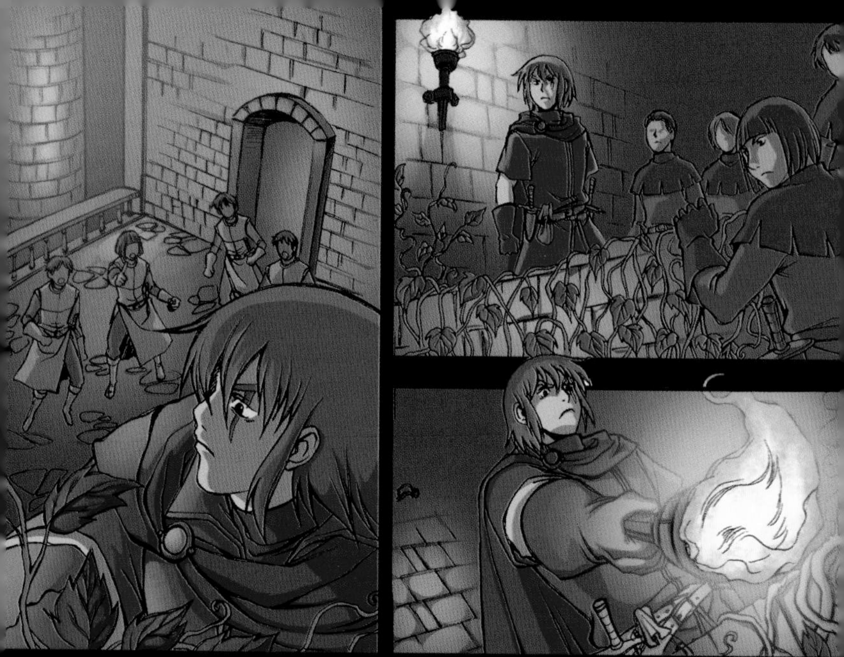



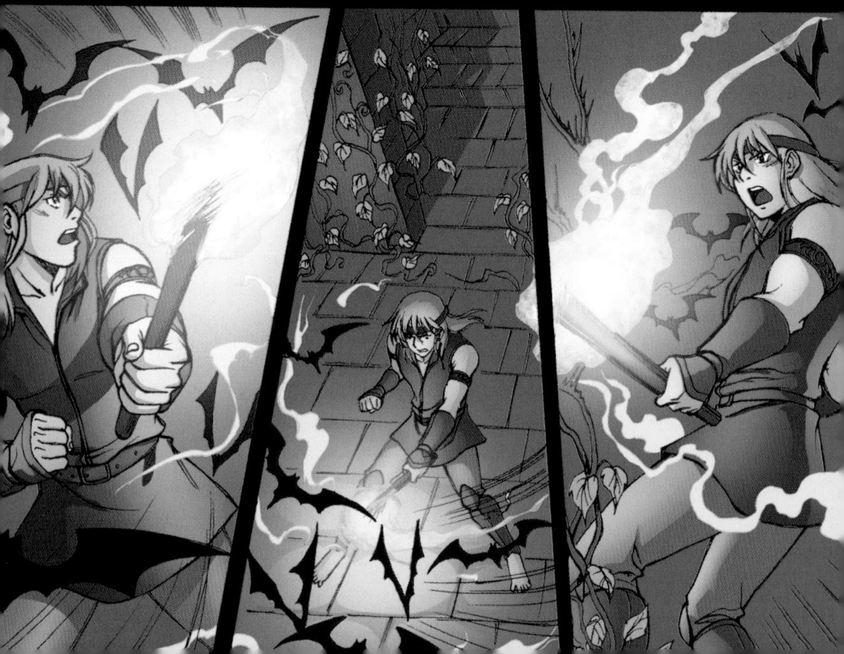

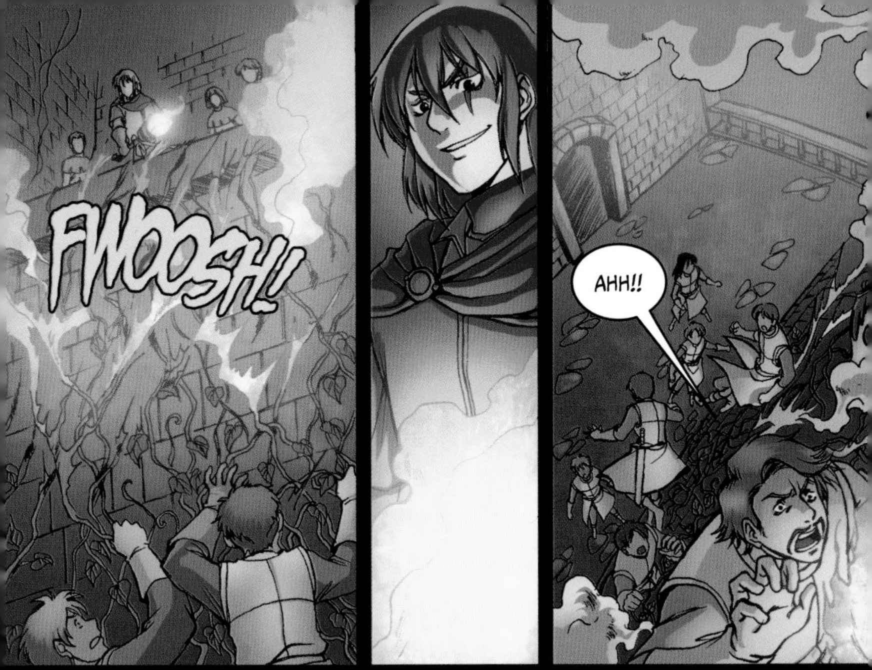
FWOOSH!!
AHH!!



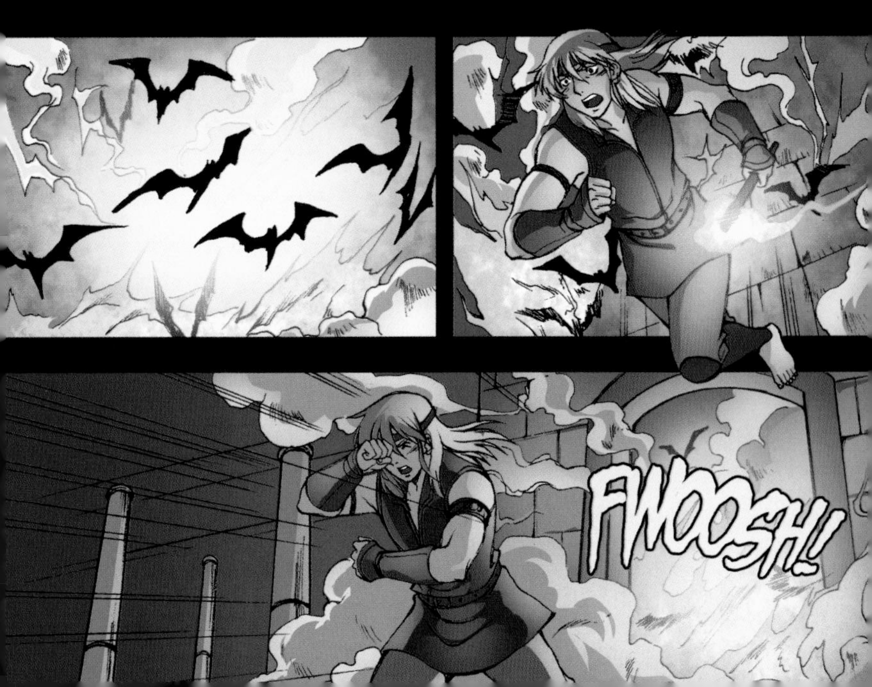
FWOOSH!!

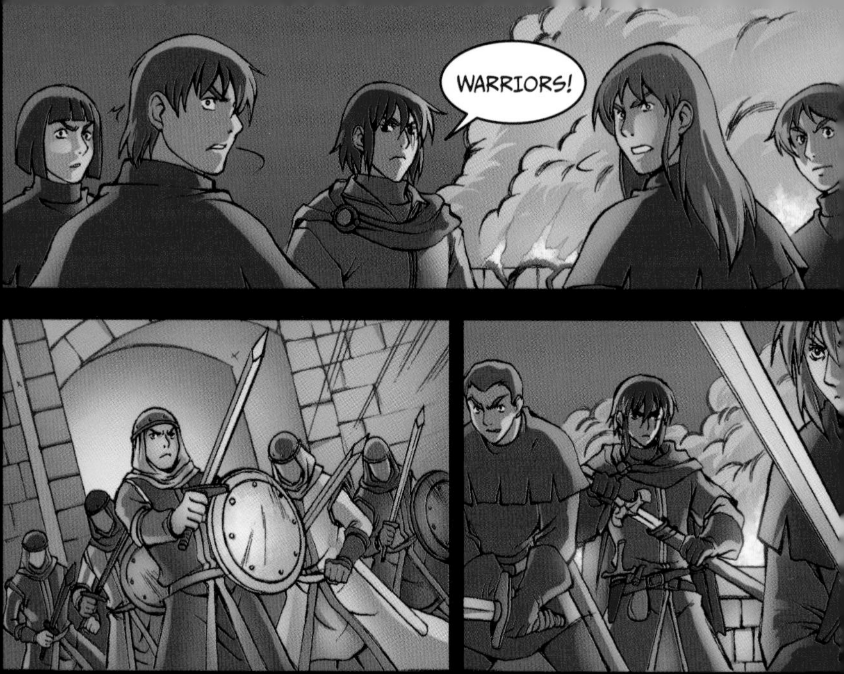
WARRIORS!



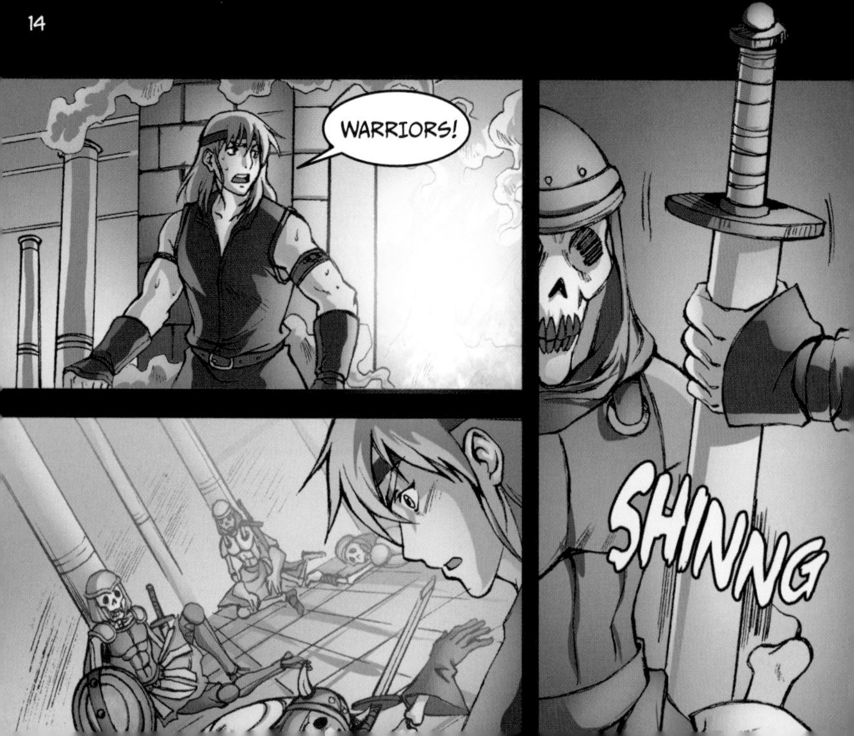
WARRIORS!
SHINNG

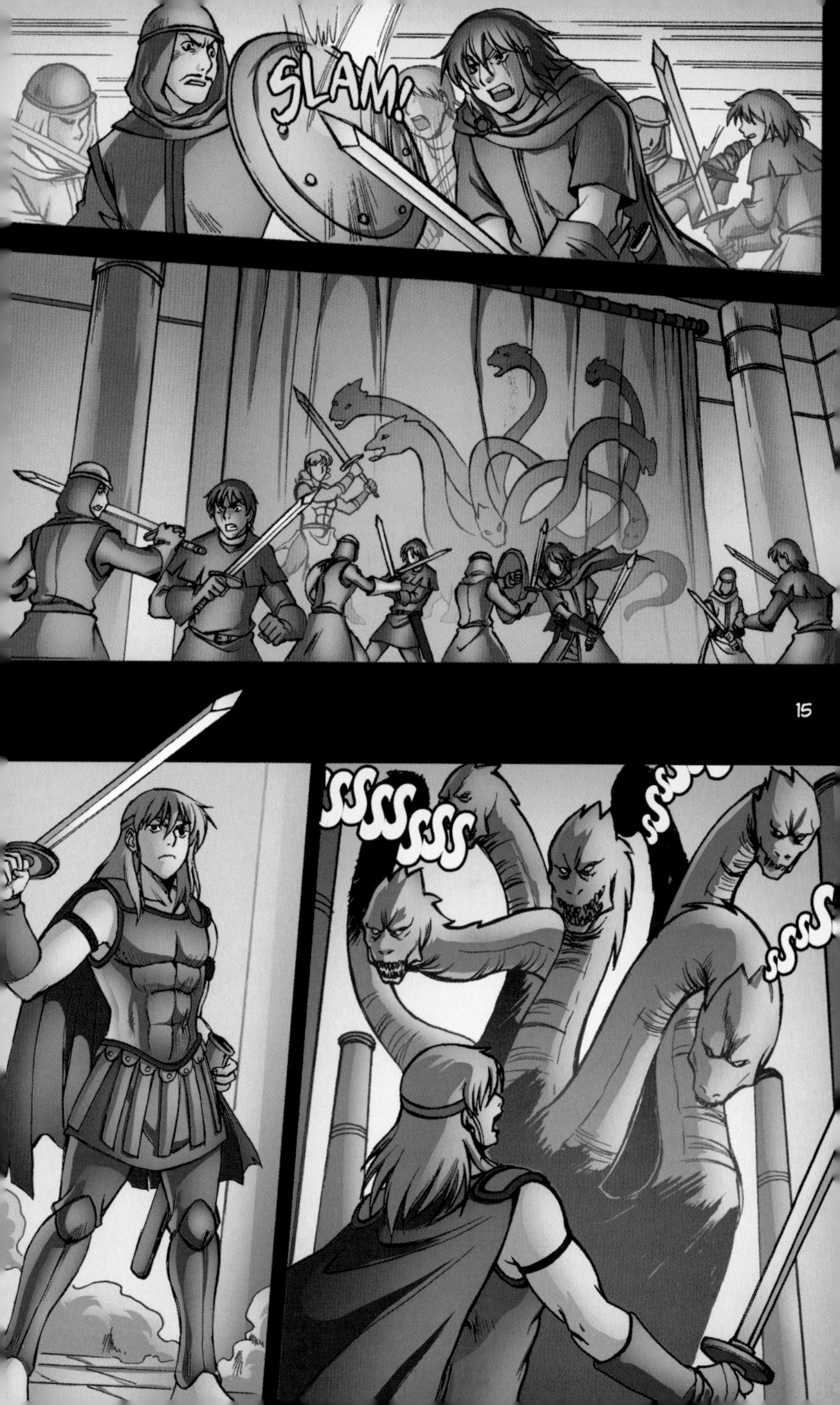
SLAM!
SSSSSSSSS
SSSS
SSSSS

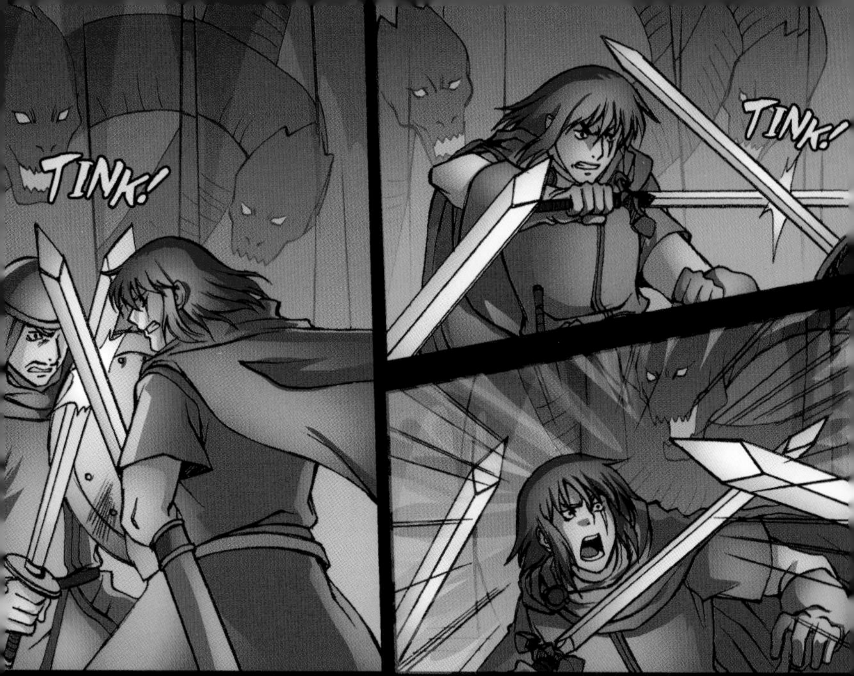
TINK!
TINK!



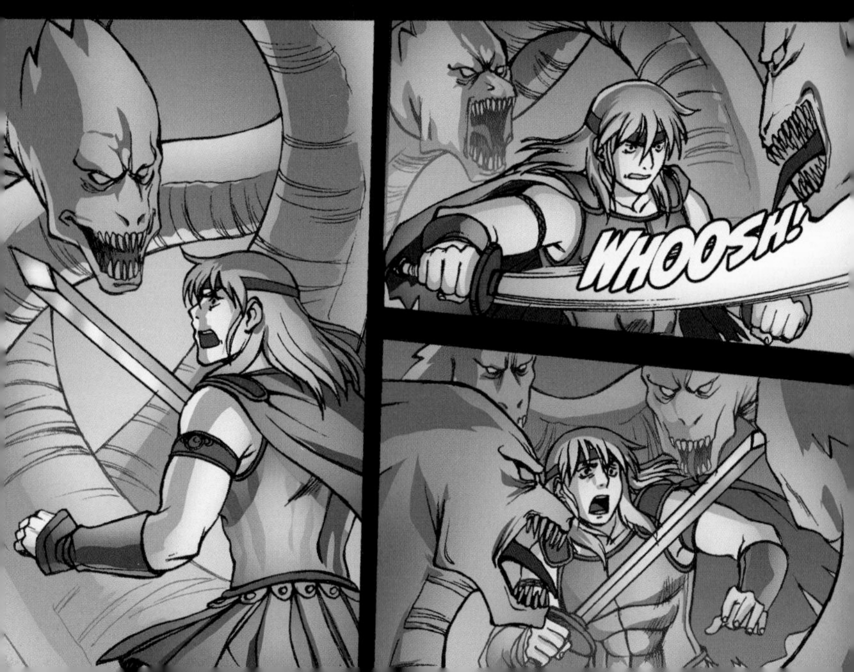
WHOOSH!

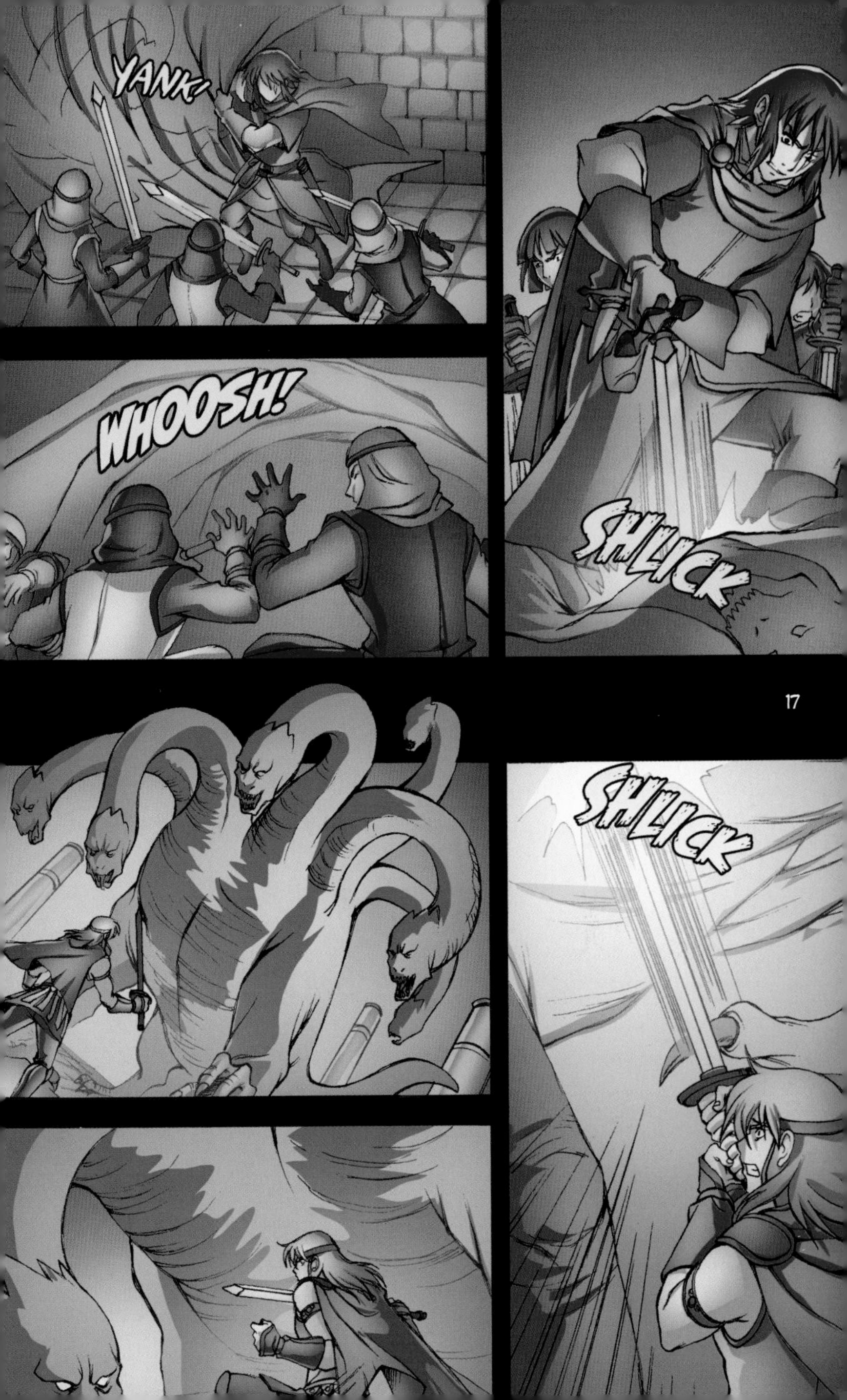
YANK!
SHLICK
WHOOSH!
SHLICK

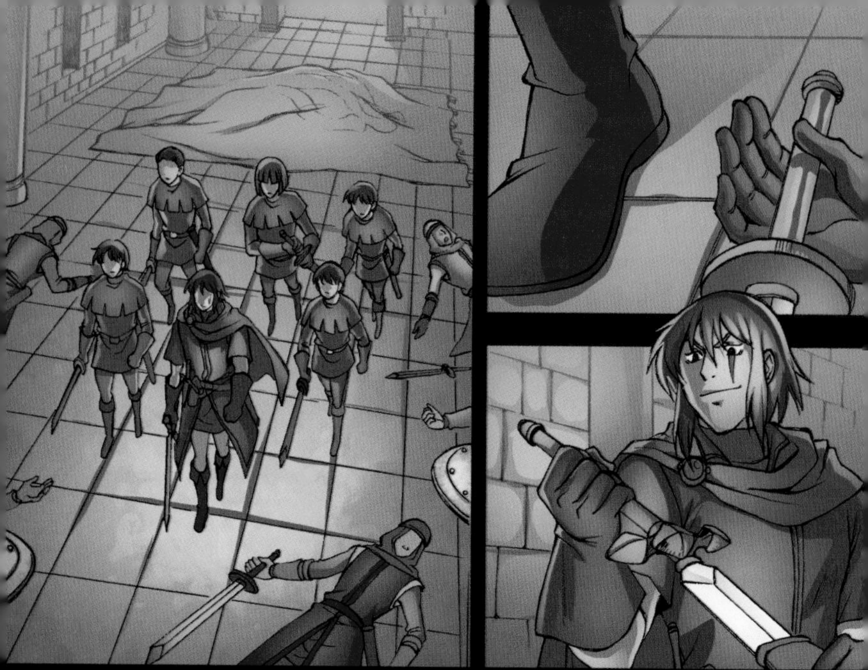



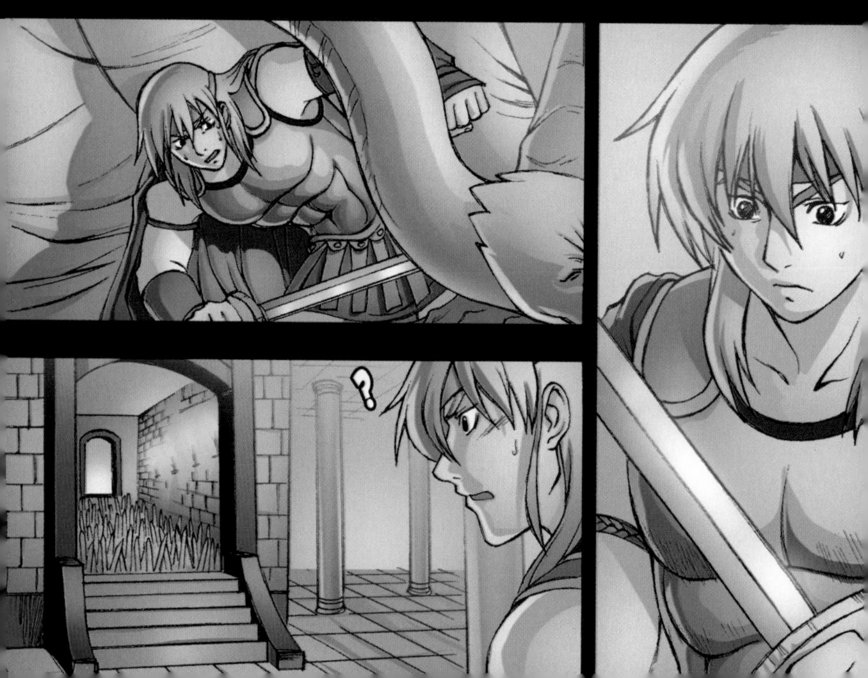

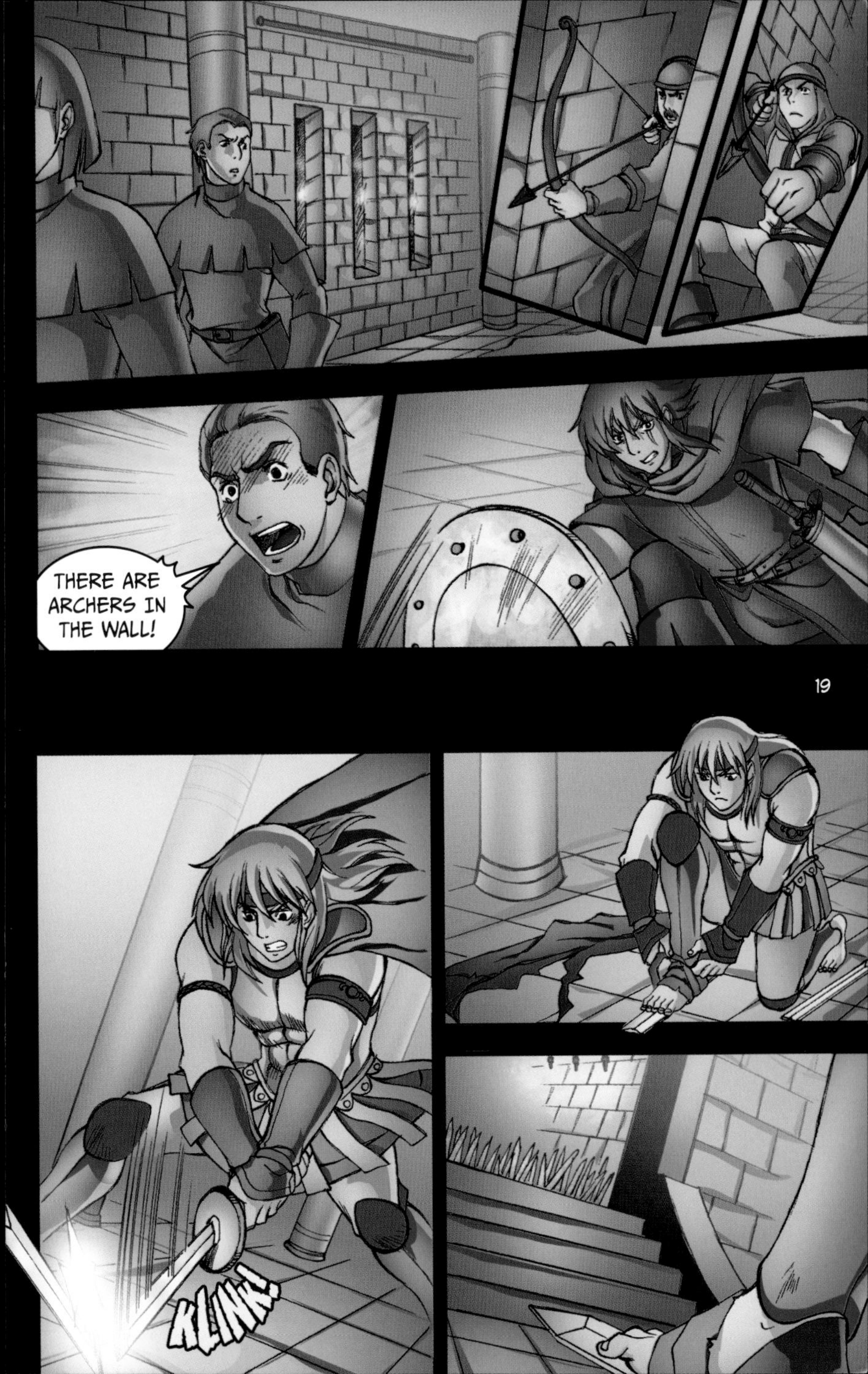
THERE ARE ARCHERS IN THE WALL!
KLINK!

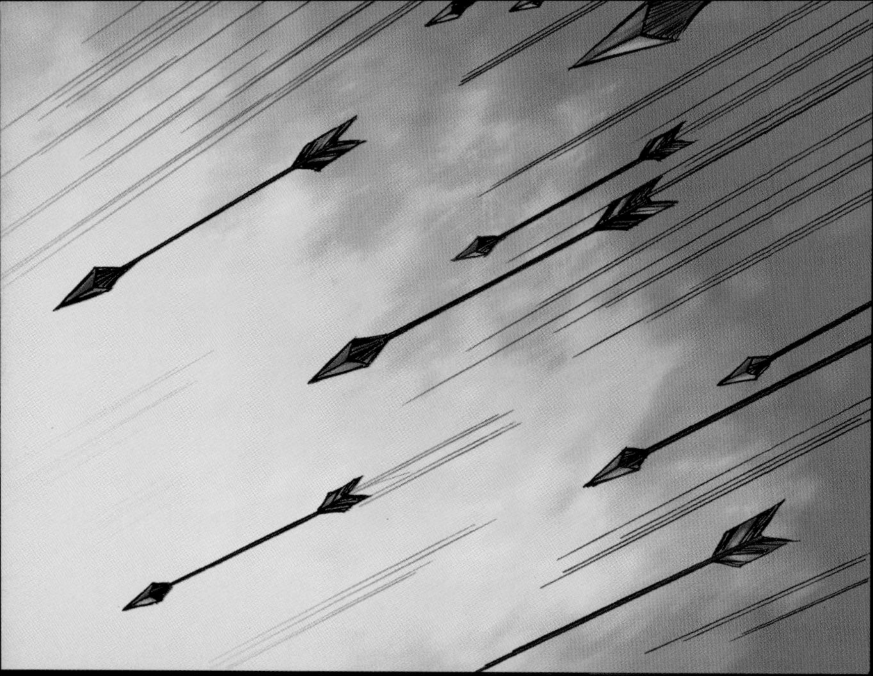



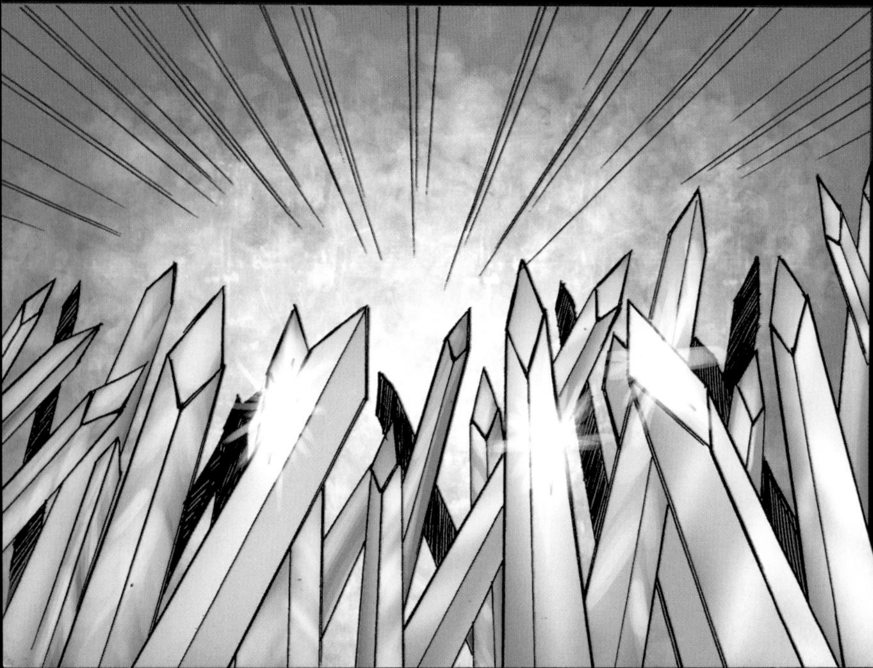

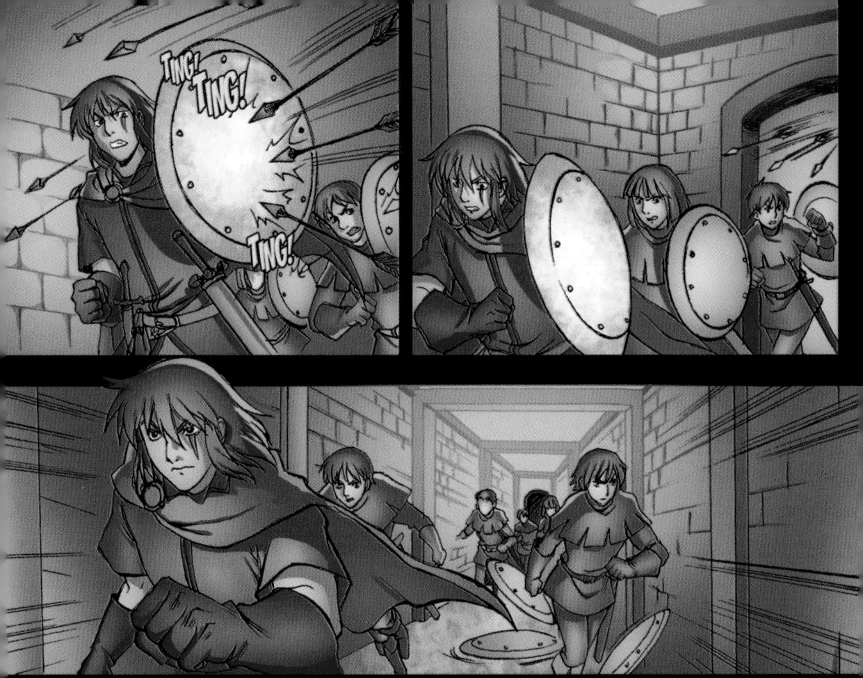
TING!
TING!
TING!



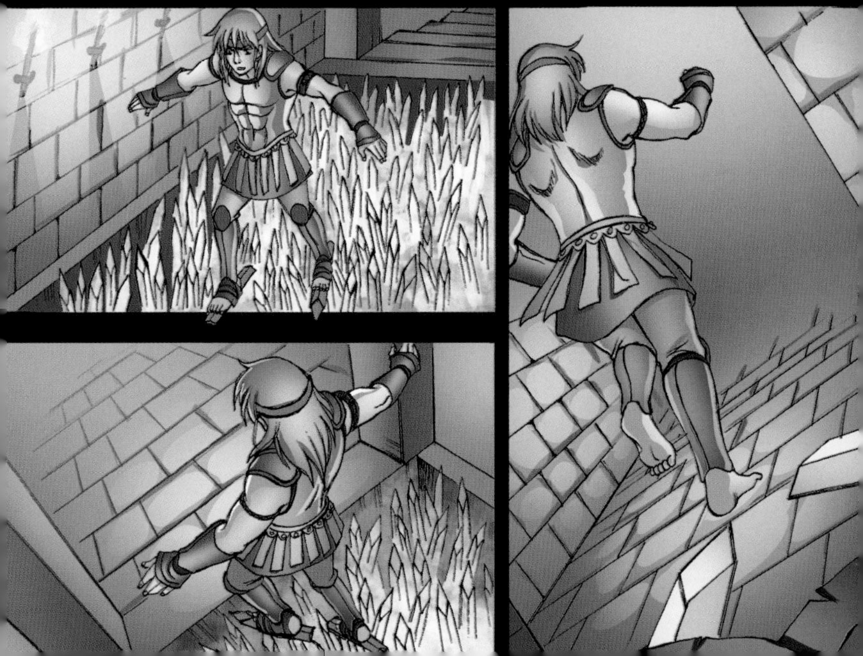

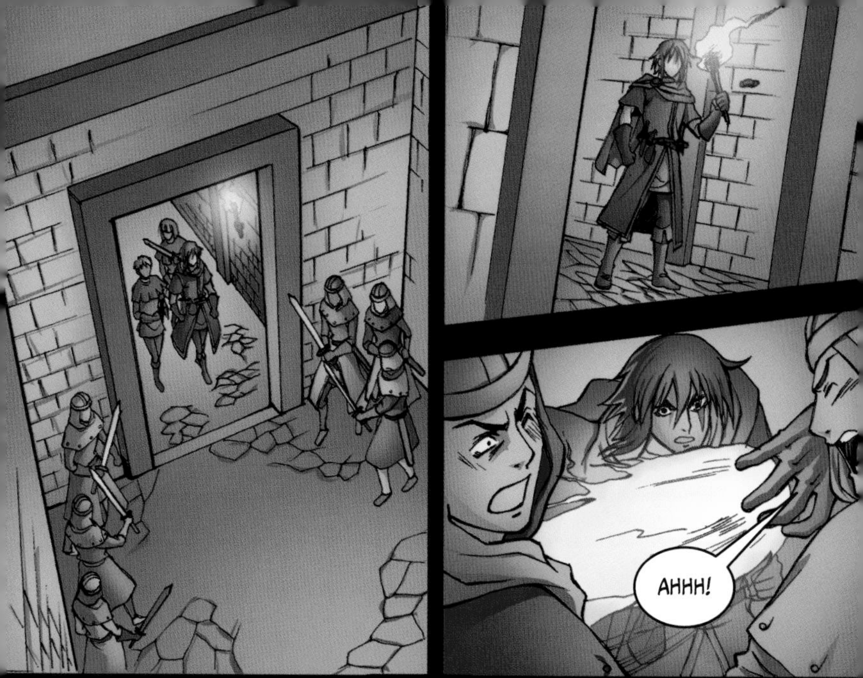
AHHH!



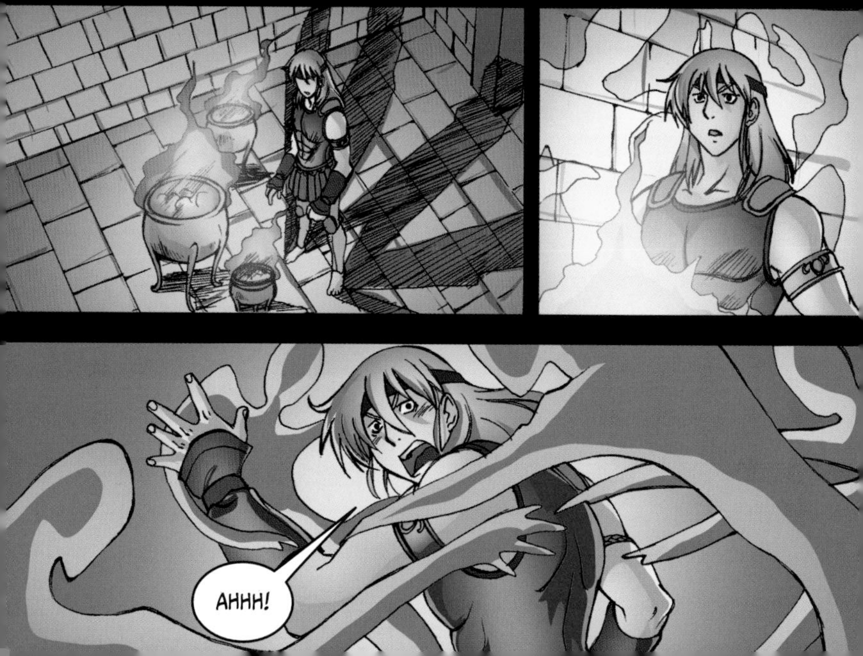
AHHH!

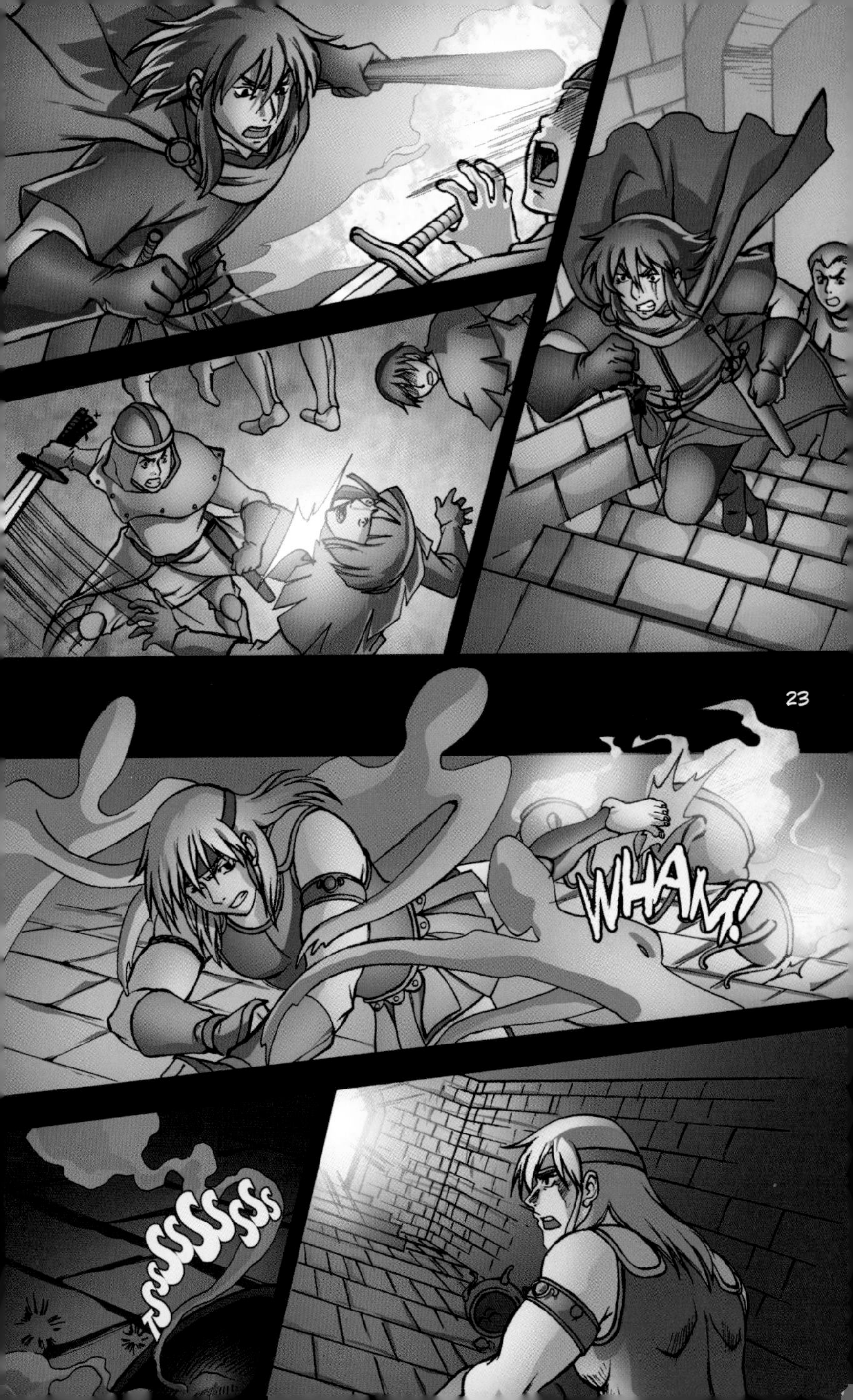
WHAM!
TSSSSSSSS

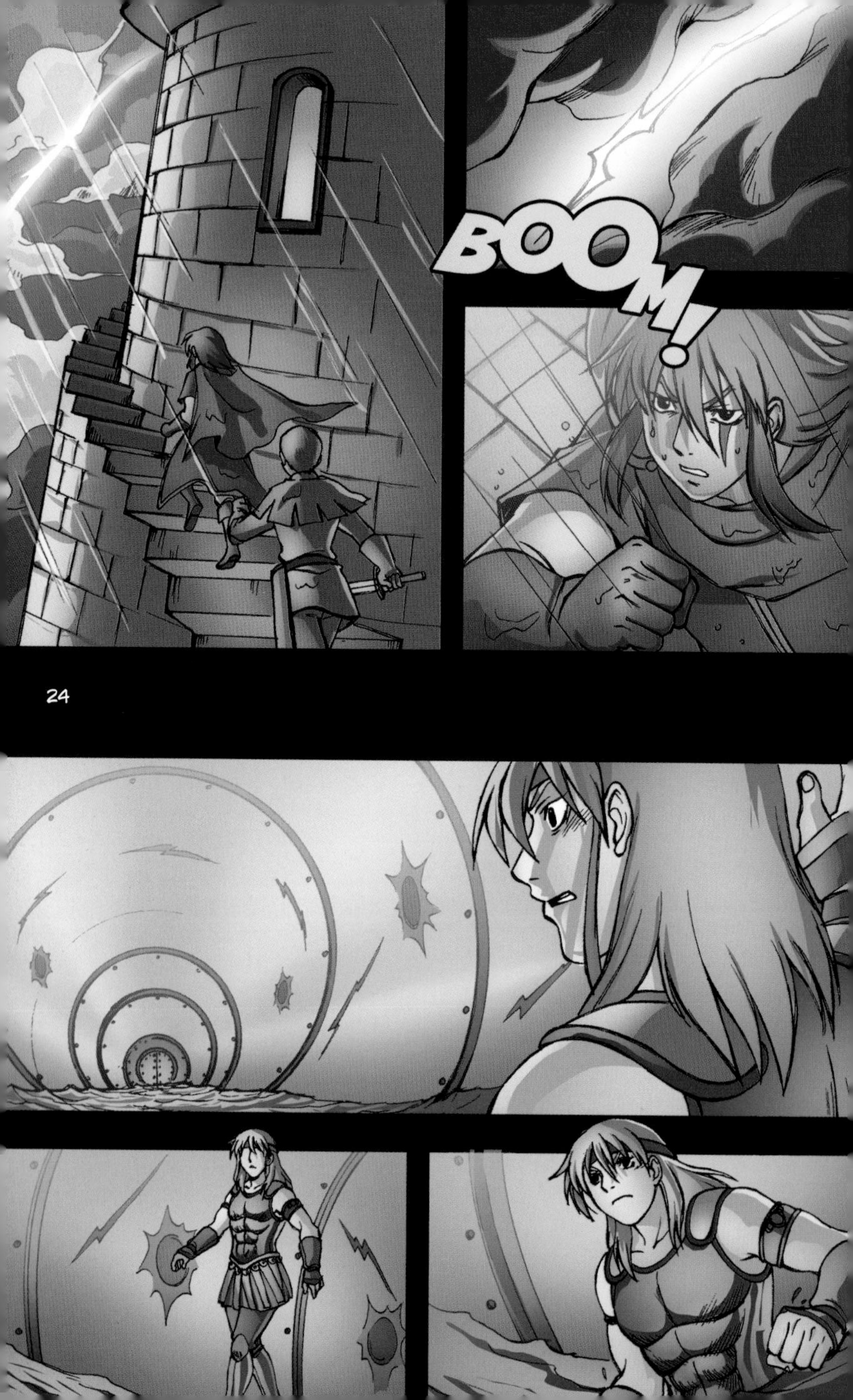
BOOM!

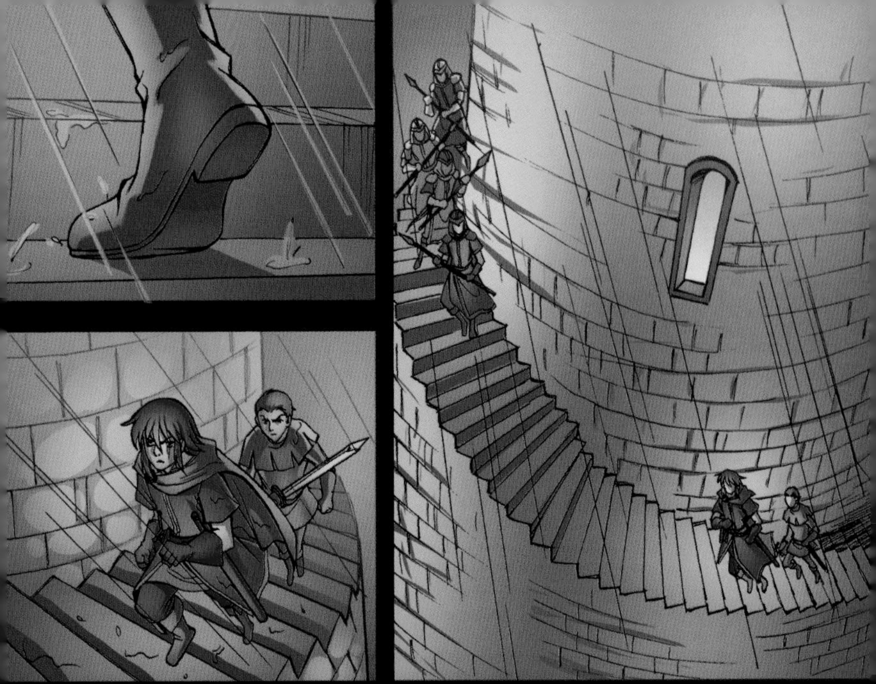



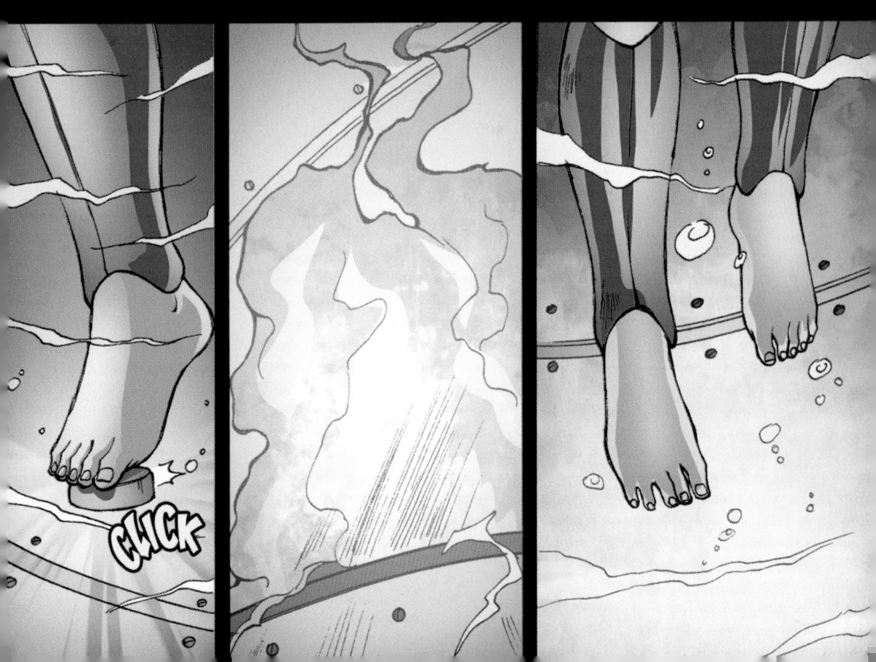
CLICK

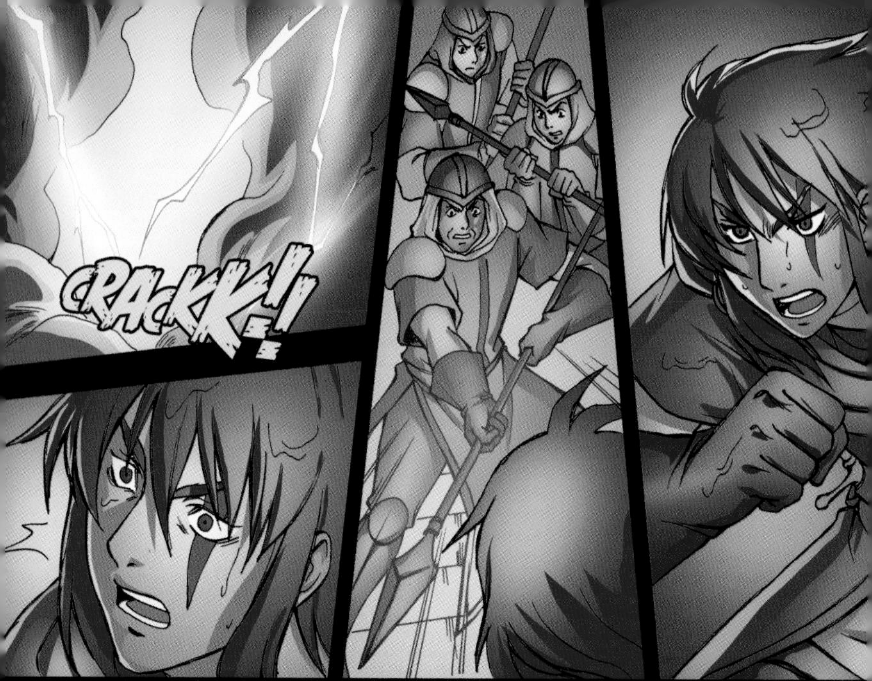
CRACKK!!



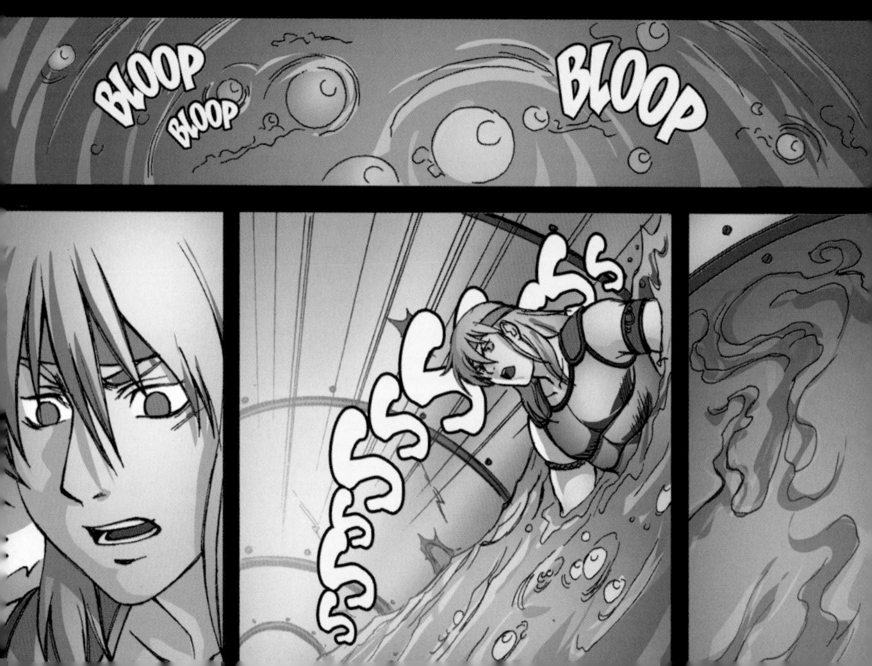
BLOOP
BLOOP
BLOOP

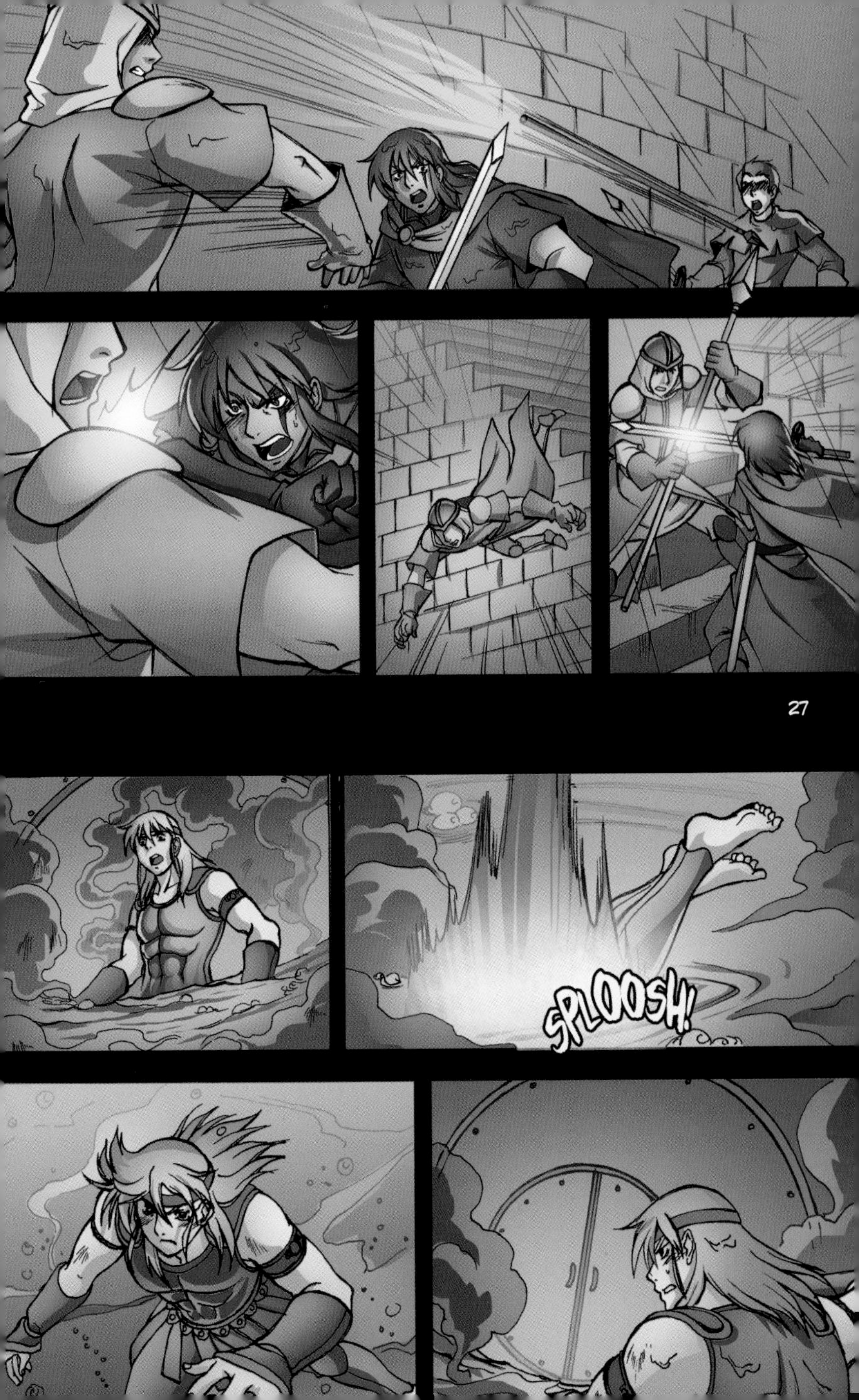
SPLOOSH!

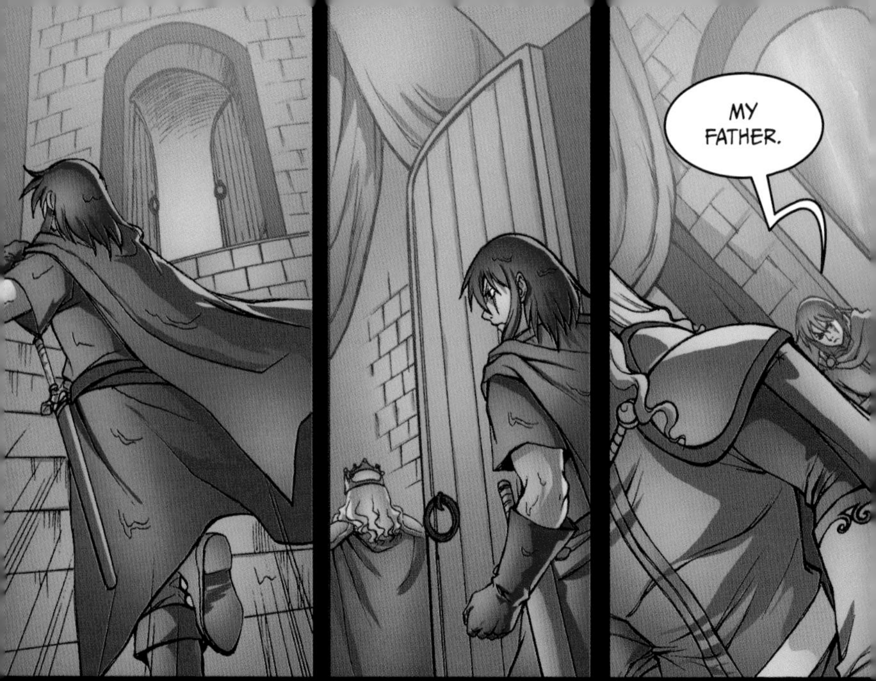
MY FATHER.



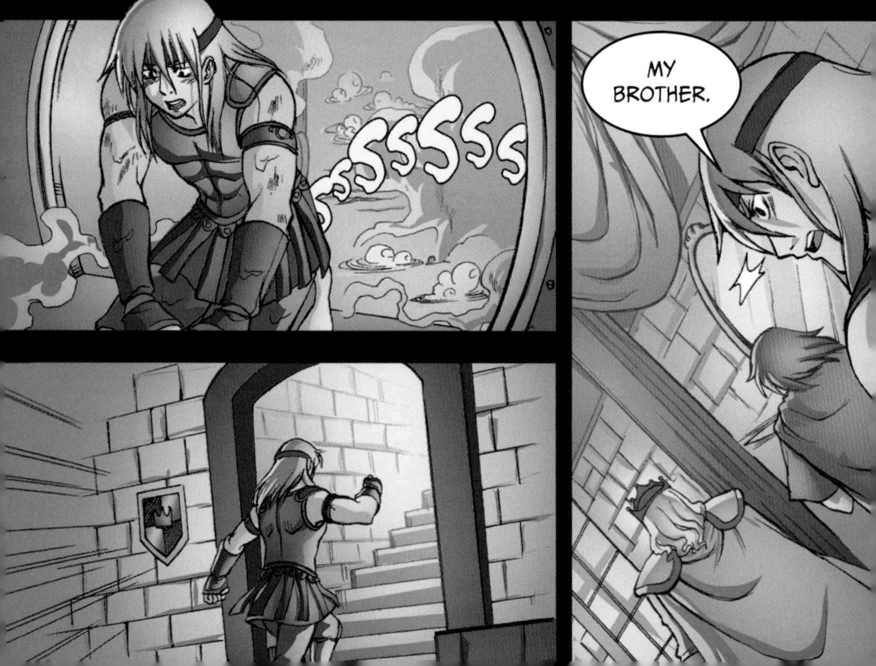
SSSSSSS
MY BROTHER.

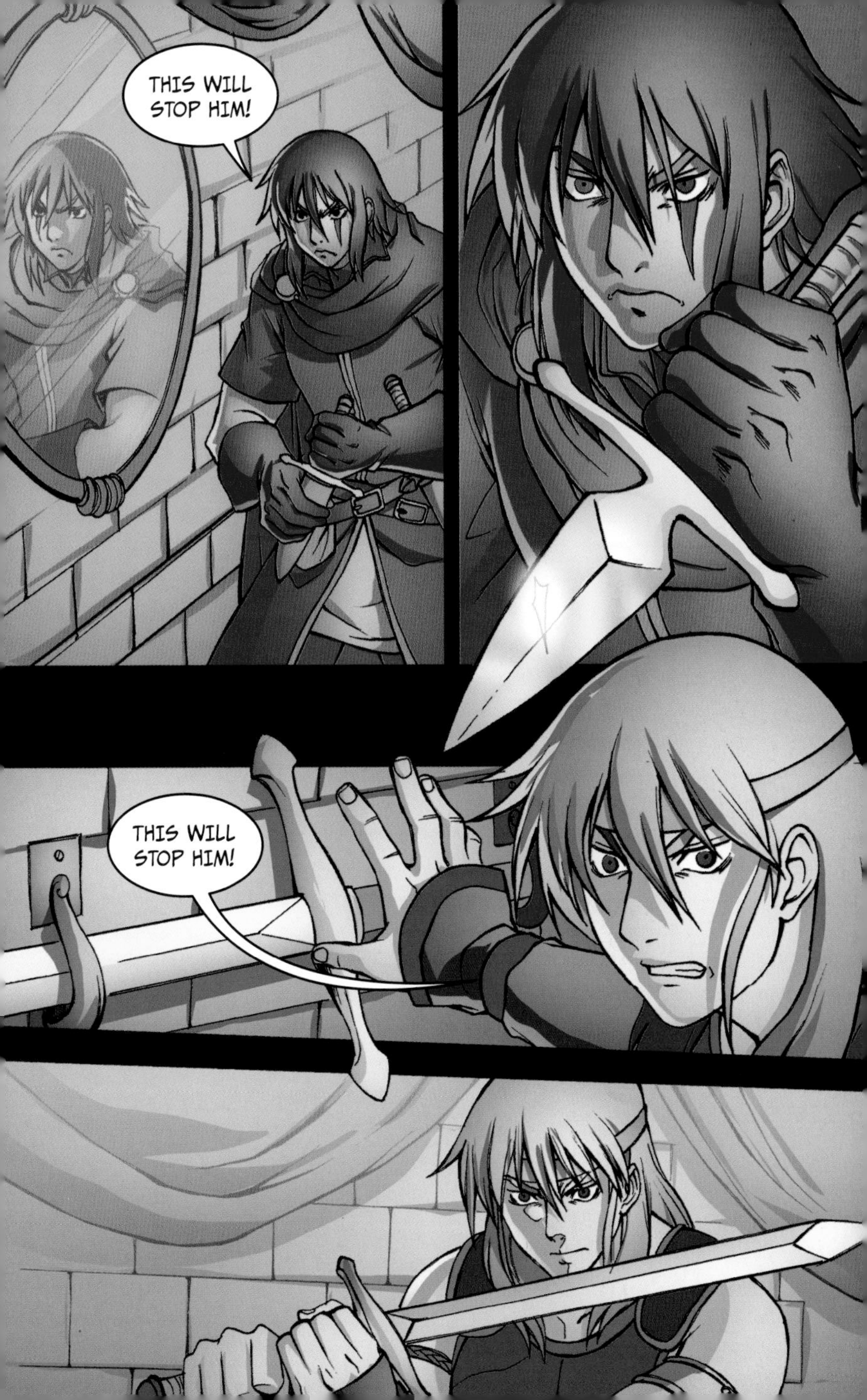
THIS WILL STOP HIM!
THIS WILL STOP HIM!

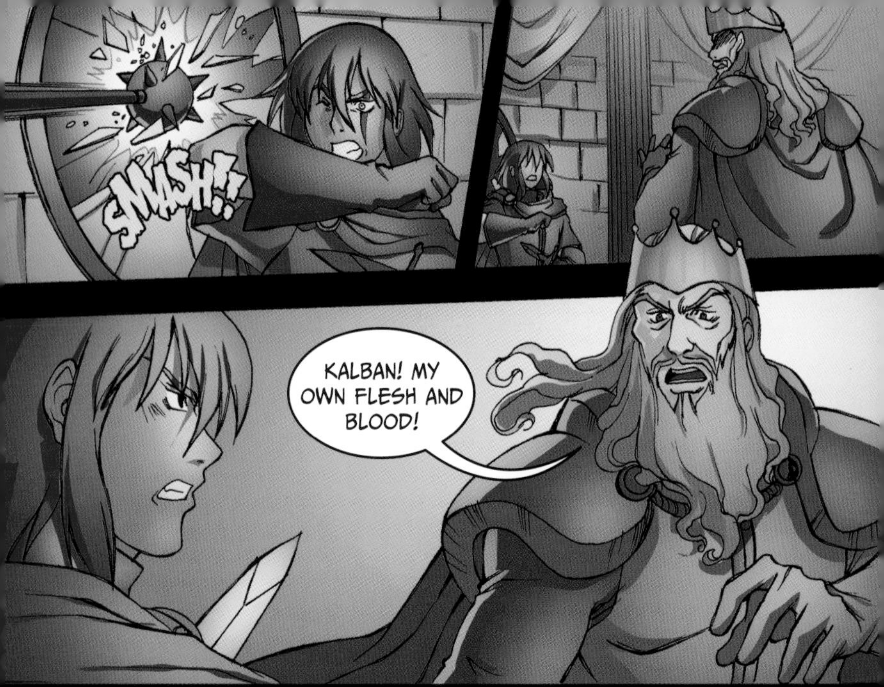
SMASH!!
KALBAN! MY OWN FLESH AND BLOOD!



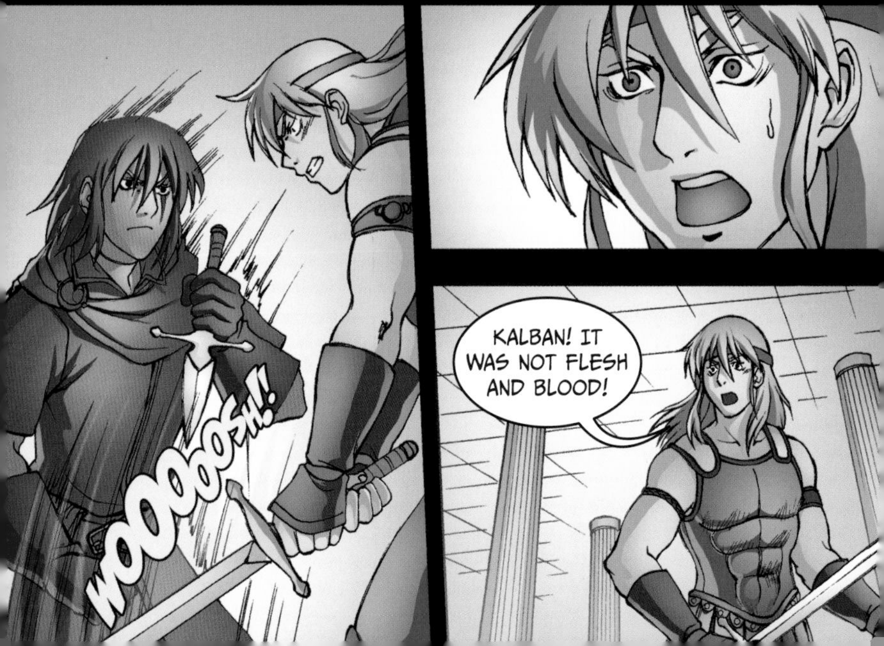
WOOOOOSH!!
KALBAN! IT WAS NOT FLESH AND BLOOD!

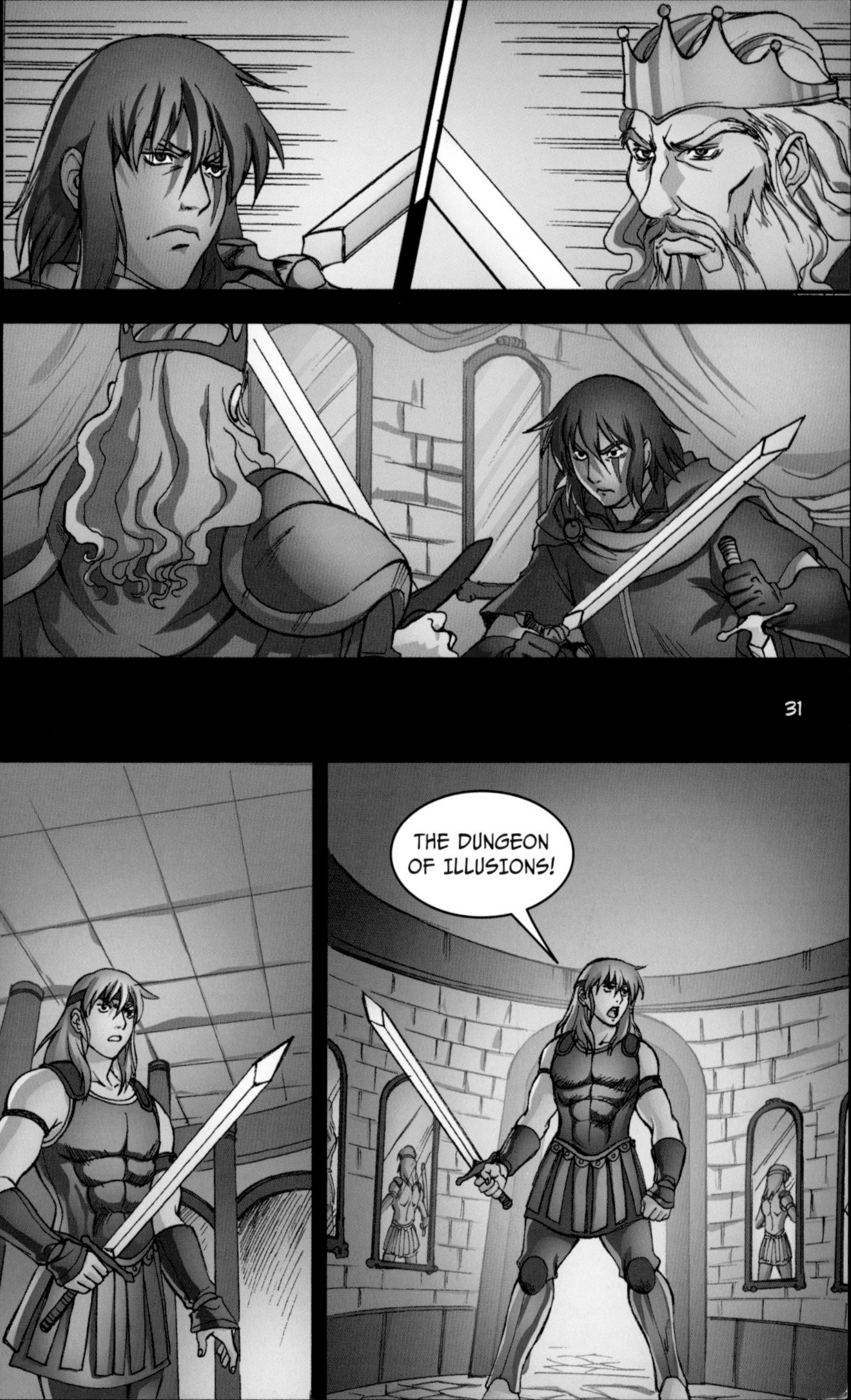
THE DUNGEON OF ILLUSIONS!

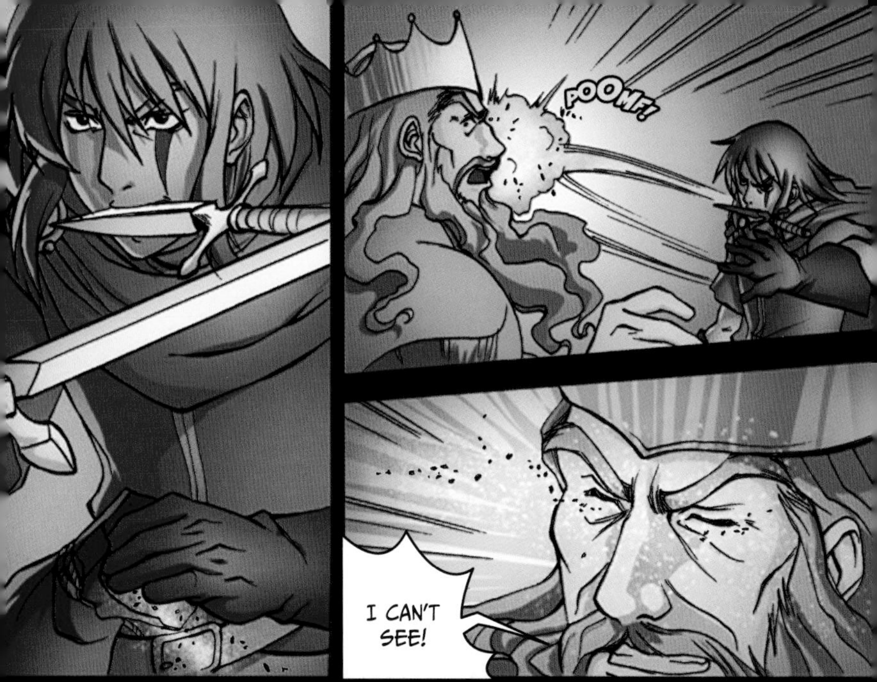
POOMF!
I CAN'T SEE!



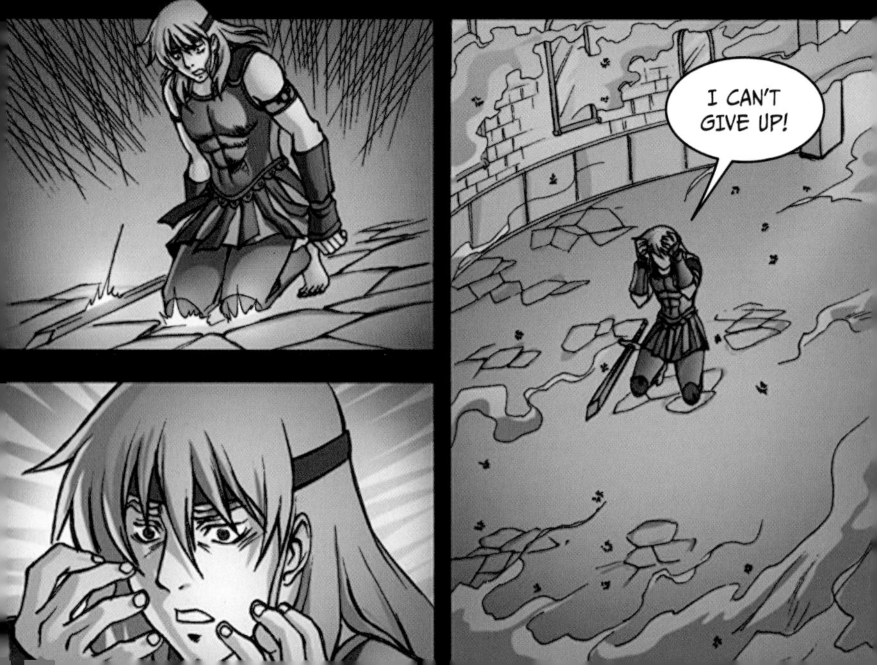
I CAN'T GIVE UP!

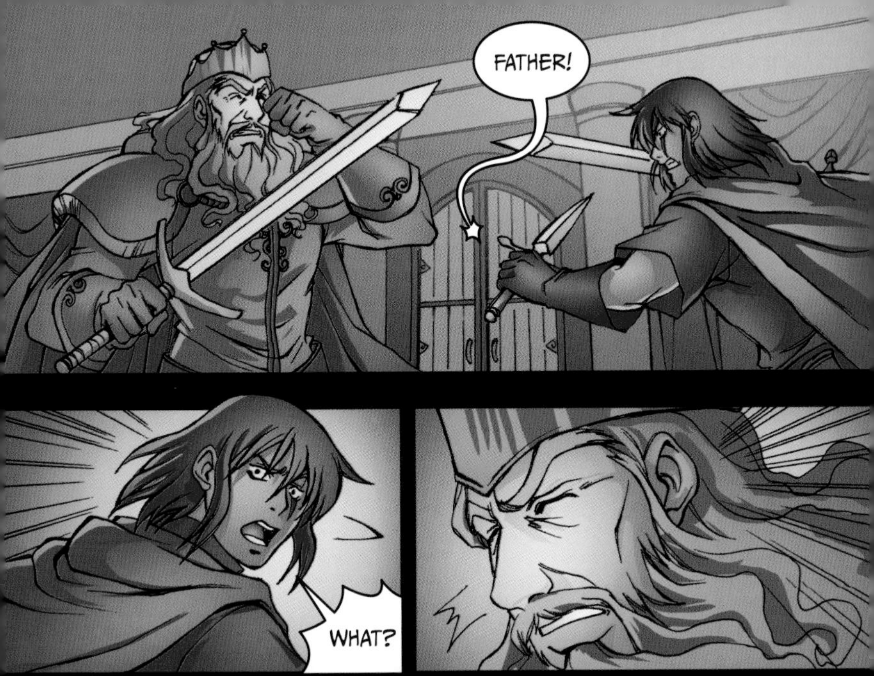
FATHER!
WHAT?



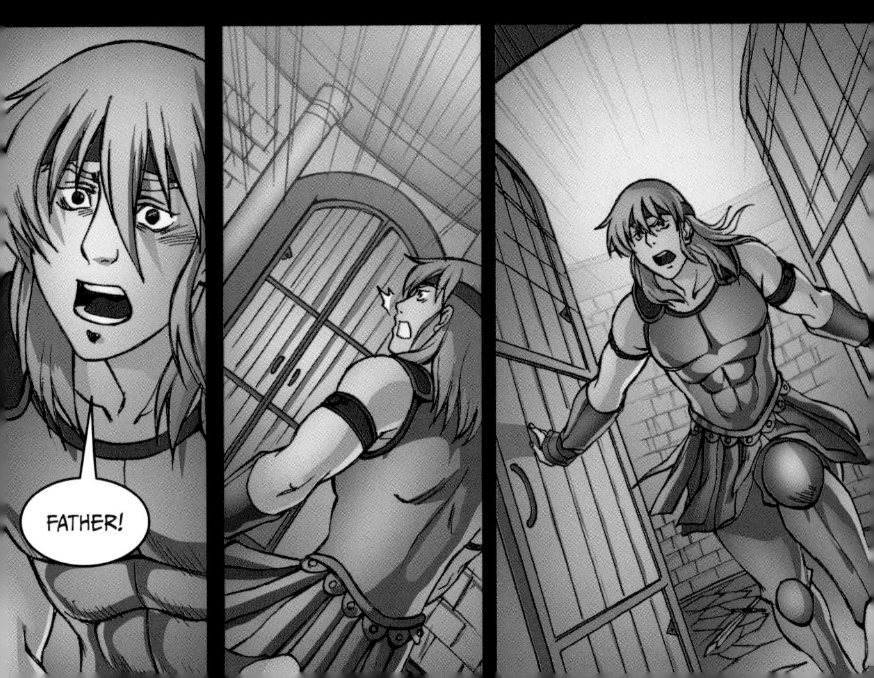
FATHER!

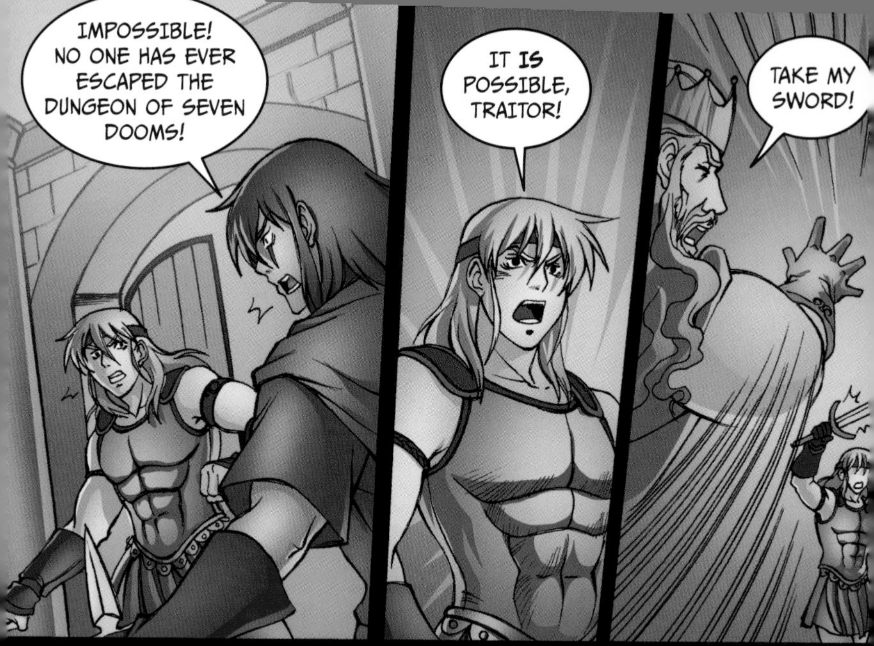
IMPOSSIBLE! NO ONE HAS EVER ESCAPED THE DUNGEON OF SEVEN DOOMS!
IT IS POSSIBLE, TRAITOR!
TAKE MY SWORD!



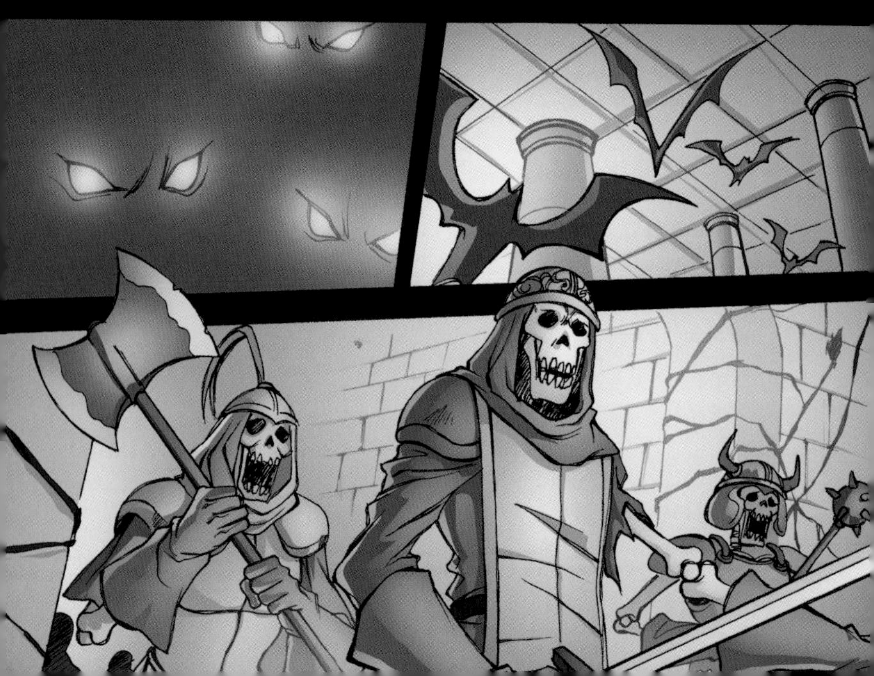

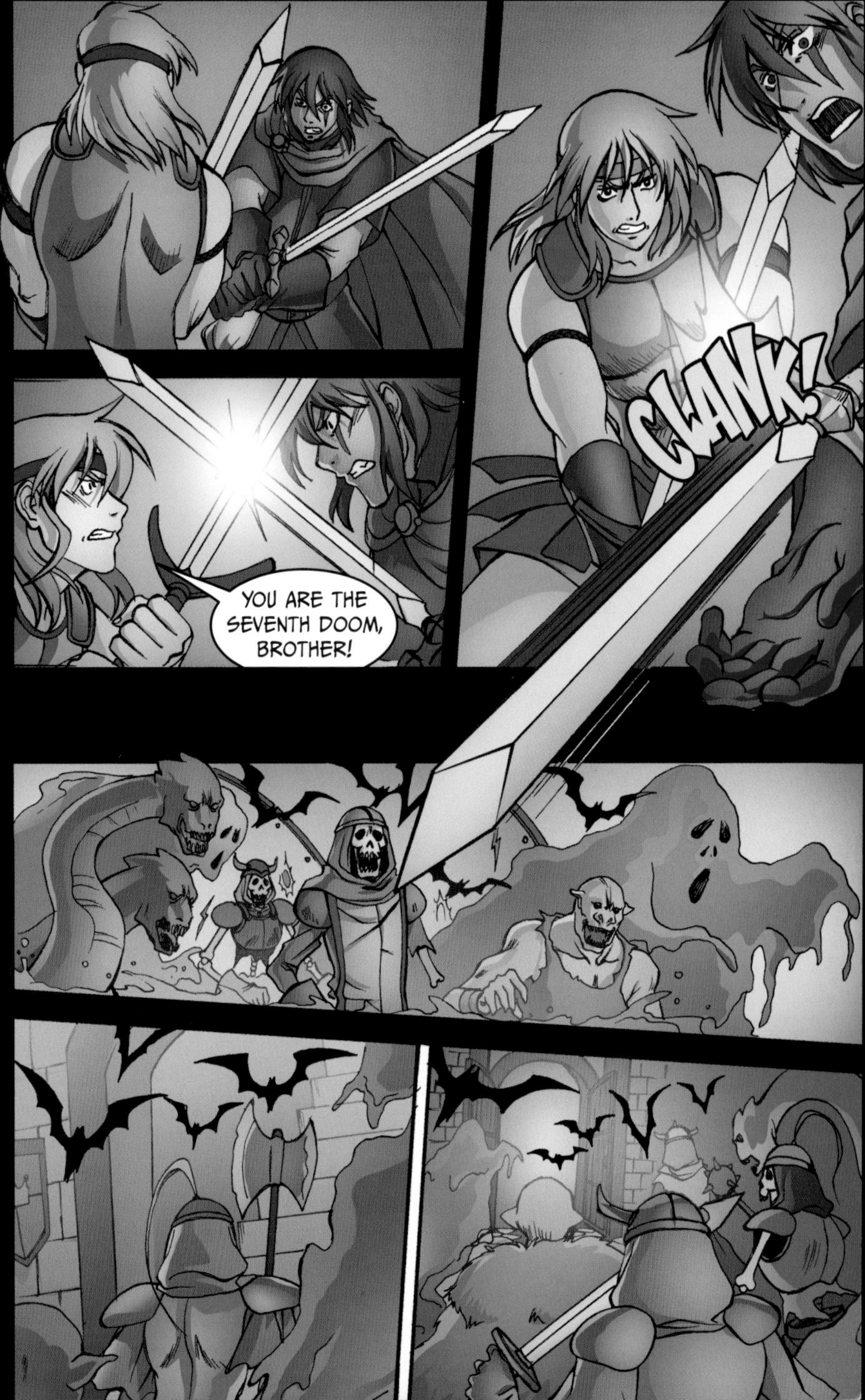
YOU ARE THE SEVENTH DOOM, BROTHER!
CLANK!

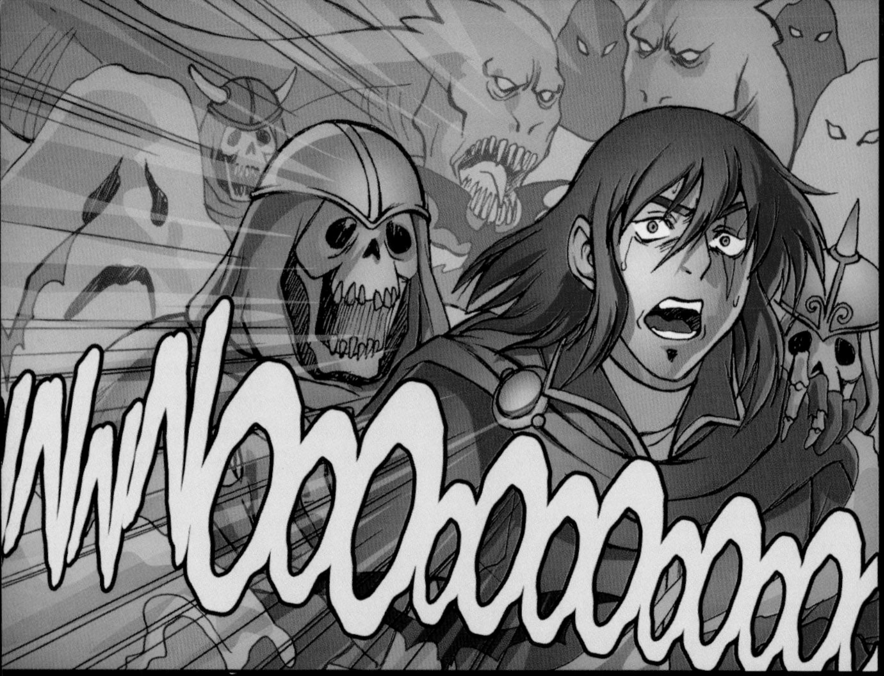
WWNOOOOOOOOOOOO



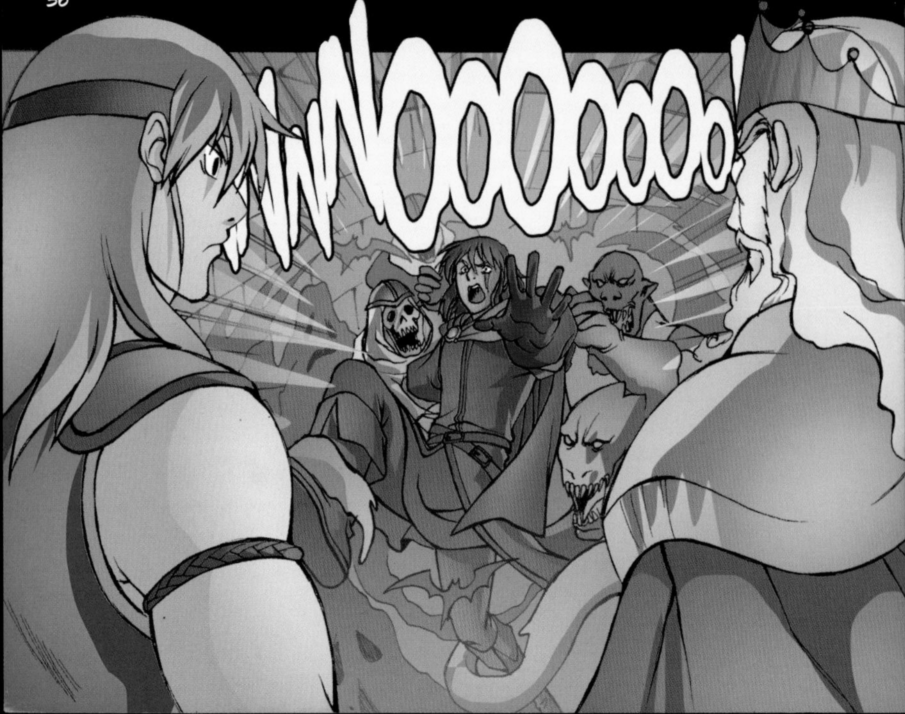
WNOOOOOOO!

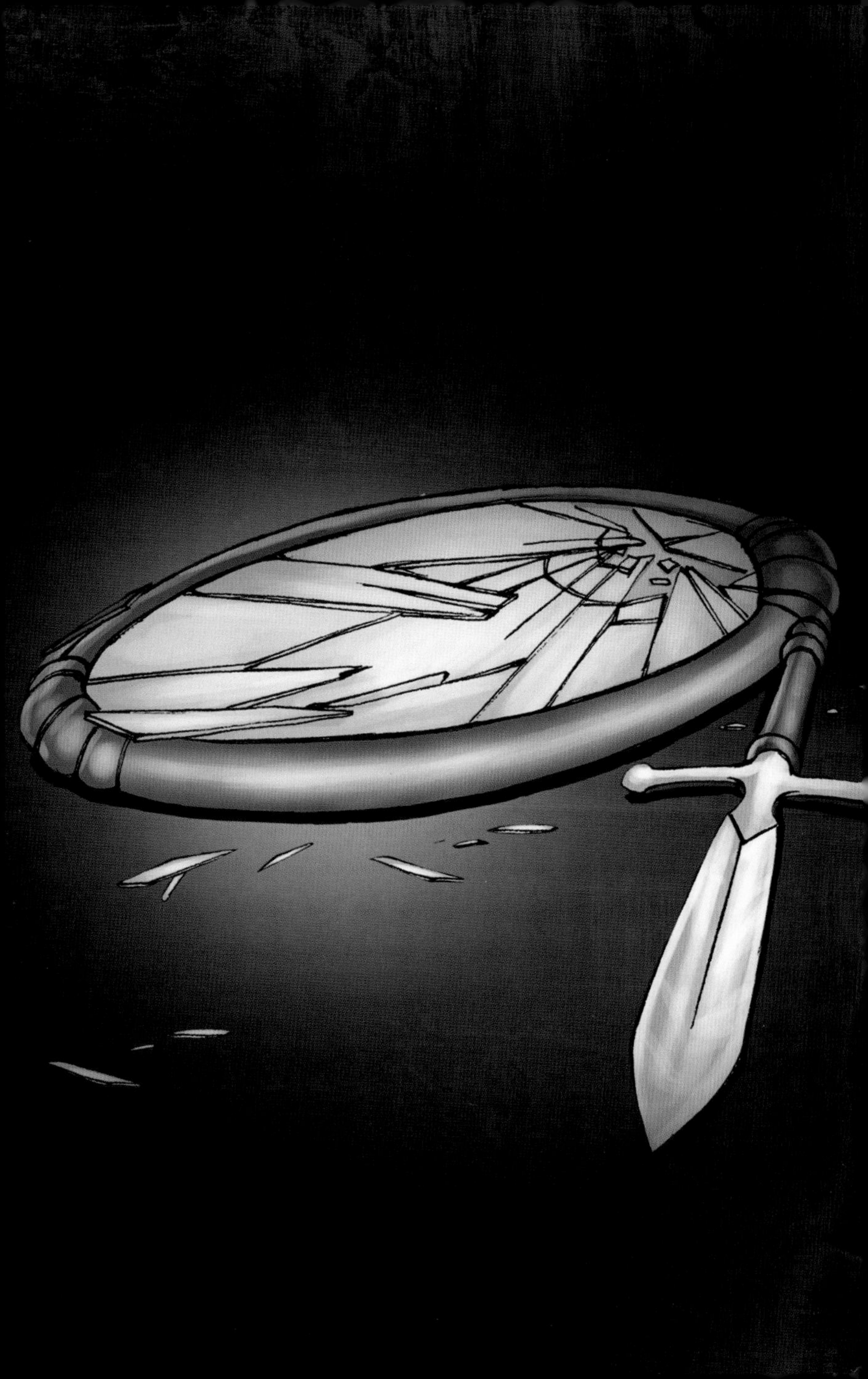

# SCRIPT BY

Michael Dahl is the author of more than 200 books for children and young adults. He has won the AEP Distinguished Achievement Award three times for his non-fiction. His Finnegan Zwake mystery series was shortlisted twice by the Anthony and Agatha awards. He has also written the Library of Doom series and the Dragonblood books. He is a featured speaker at conferences around the country on graphic novels and high-interest books for boys.

# VISUAL GLOSSARY

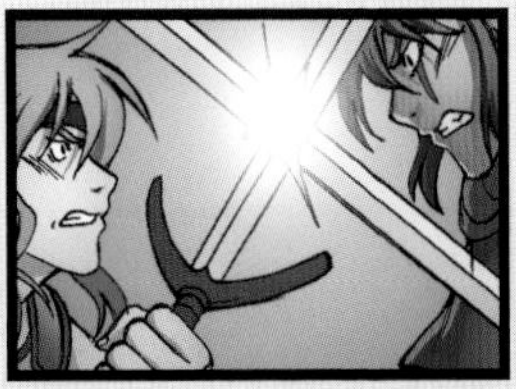

## SWORD FIGHTS

In a graphic novel, even noise can be shown visually. During the sword flights, bursts of light show us that the swords have connected and that the blades are making a bright, metallic sound.

## THE HYDRA

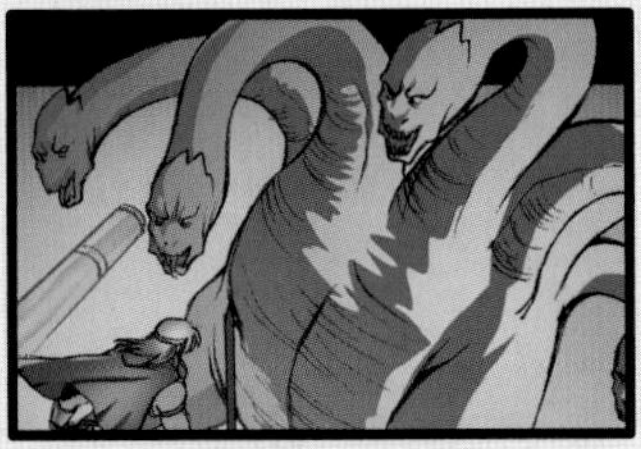

Authors and illustrators often include characters or ideas from other people's stories in their own work. The seven-headed dragon, or Hydra, comes from the ancient Greek myth of Hercules.

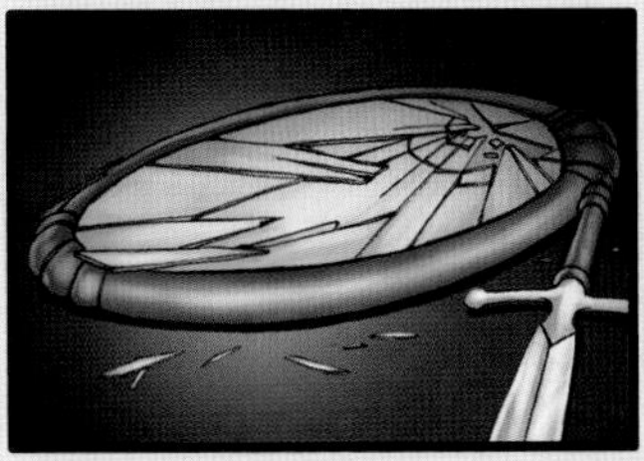

## BROKEN MIRROR

A single object can symbolize more than one meaning. The broken mirror at the end of the story can show the outcome of a battle, or tell us that an image, or illusion, has been destroyed.

## THE FALLING TAPESTRY

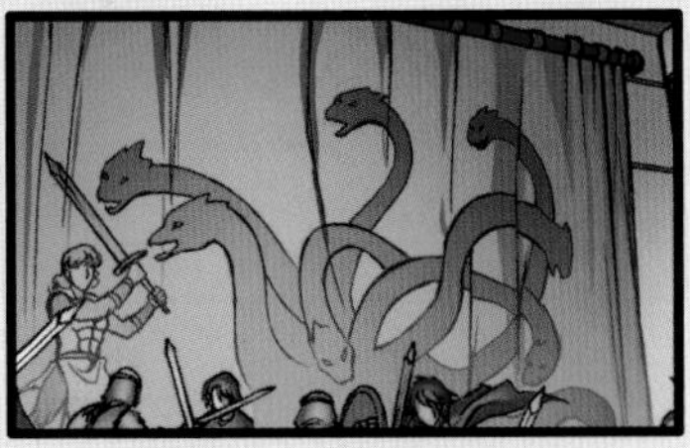

Graphic novels use parallel, or side-by-side action to compare things we normally would not consider. Could being buried under a gigantic carpet feel like being crushed by a monster?

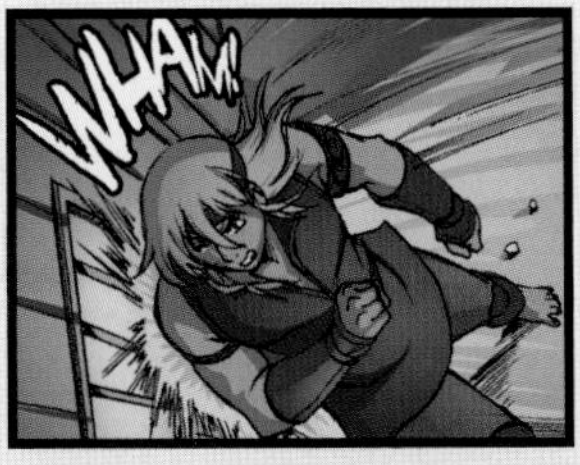
WHAM!

## ACTION LINES

Action lines in graphic novels indicate speed, force, or intense emotion – or all three at once. We know that Prince Arel has hit the locked door with great force because of the lines that flow out from him, and because of the burst between his shoulder and the door itself.

# VISUAL QUESTIONS

1. This adventure is titled *Dungeon of Seven Dooms.* Each doom is introduced visually throughout Prince Arel's journey. Can you locate all seven dangers?

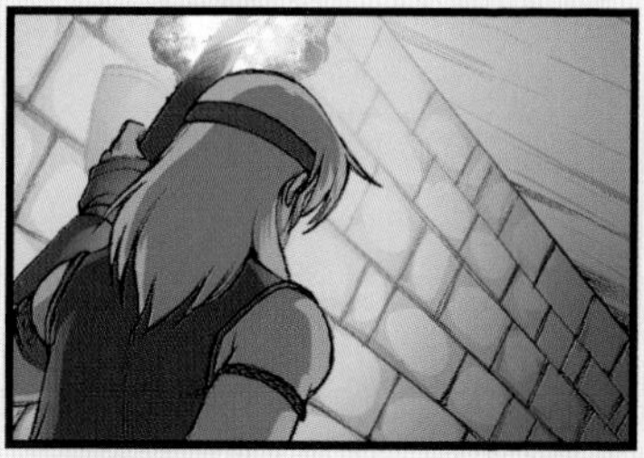

2. Although the twin princes face parallel dangers, they take different paths. Kalban avoids arrows from above using a shield. Arel overcomes blades from below by destroying his own sword. What do their different actions tell us about the brothers?

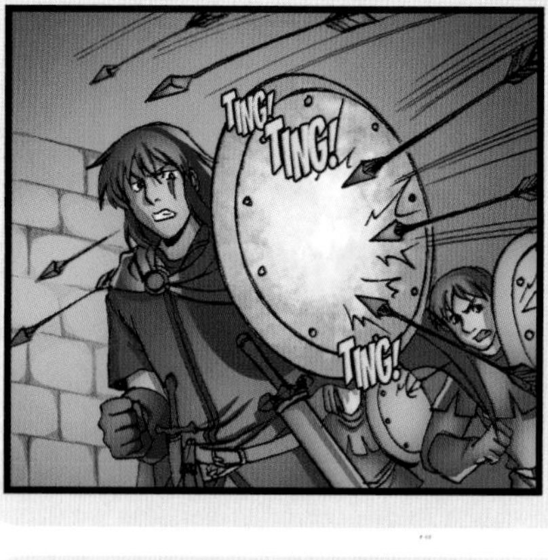
TING!
TING!
TING!

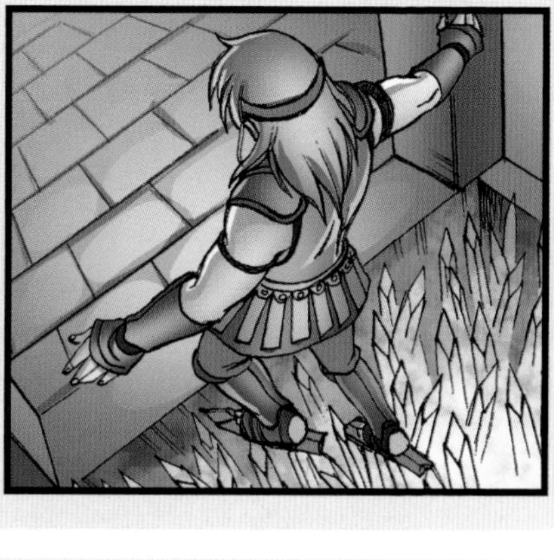

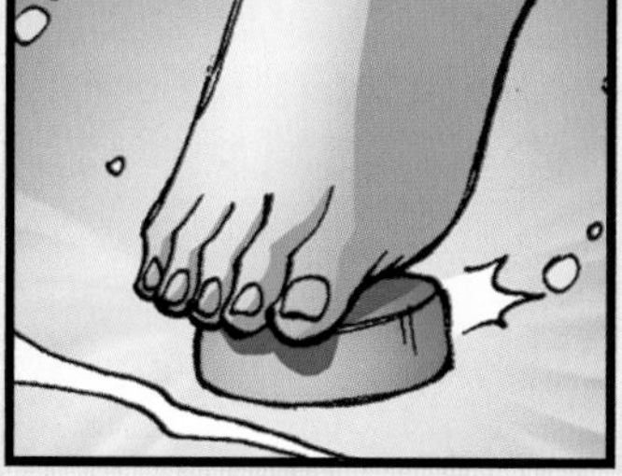

3. When Arel enters the metal chamber filled with water, he steps on a button and activates a hidden mechanism. Visual clues in the following panels tell you something is happening to the water. What?

4. The evil prince is about to strike down the king, but he stops. The panel shows him turning around. Why? And can you tell from the illustrations what he is feeling?

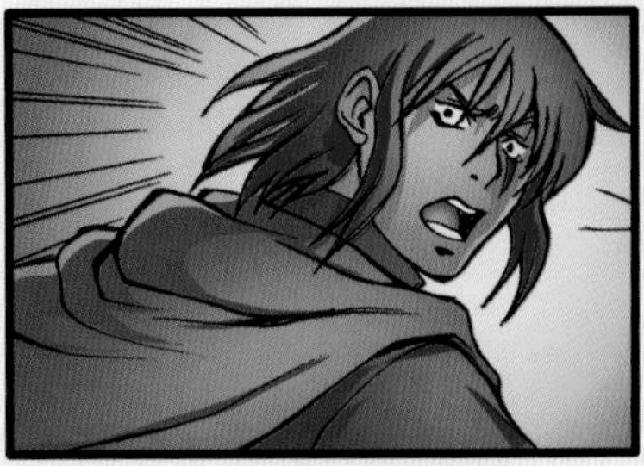

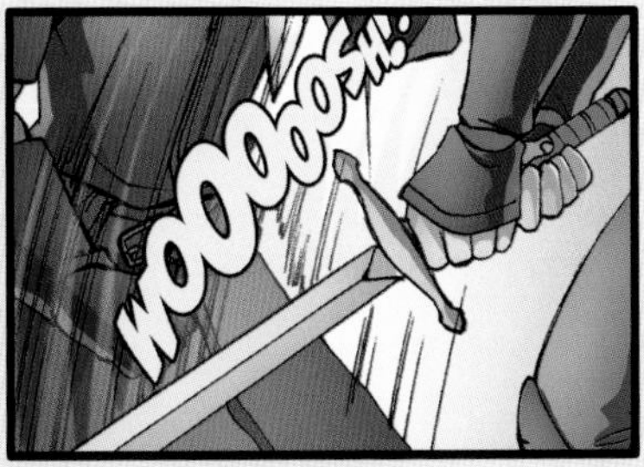
WOOOOOSH!!

5. Arel's sword seems to pass harmlessly through Kalban. Why? Do the following panels hint at where Arel is? Do they explain why Kalban was not harmed?

6. As the evil Kalban is dragged down into the dungeons, the illustrator has represented all seven dooms in the artwork. Can you identify them all?

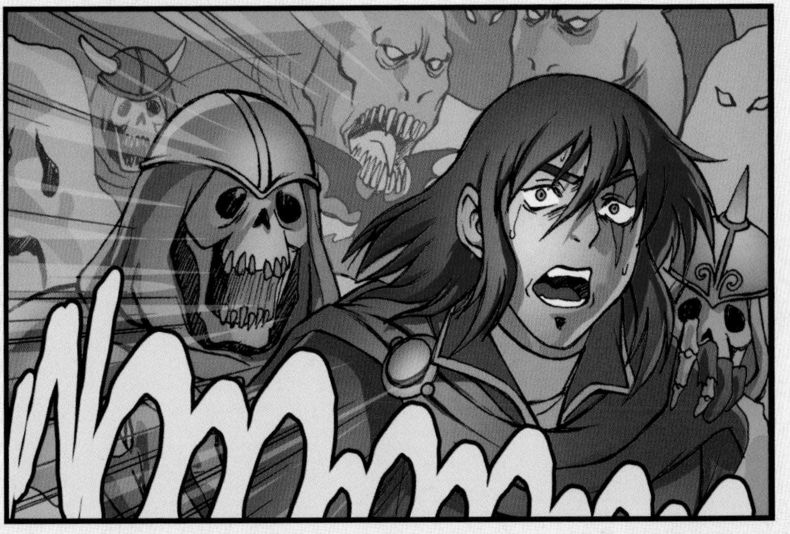

# CREATING THE BOOK

## THE MANUSCRIPT

Graphic novels are often created by two different people —
a writer and an illustrator. Even when a book contains few
words, the writer must provide detailed notes called "scene
descriptions," instructing the content of each panel.

A page from the *Dungeon of Seven Dooms* manuscript:

Page 12

UPPER
Panel 1
KALBAN looks down and sees some palace guards
looking up at him and his men from the terrace below.
The guards are pointing and obviously angered at the evil
prince's attack on the king's private quarters.

Panel 2
KALBAN and his henchmen reach the top of the wall.
They are swinging over the edge of the terrace they were
climbing toward.

Panel 3
KALBAN takes a nearby torch and lights the vines.

LOWER
Panel 1
AREL swings his torch at the bats.

Panel 2
Another angle of AREL fighting off the bats. He is trying
to inch his way through the chamber of vines and bats.

Panel 3
AREL's torch lights the vines. Many of them begin to
burn and smoke.

## PENCILS

After receiving the manuscript from the writer, the illustrator creates rough sketches called "pencils." The writer and editor of the book review these drawings, making sure all corrections are made before continuing to the next stage.

From page 12 of *Dungeon of Seven Dooms*:

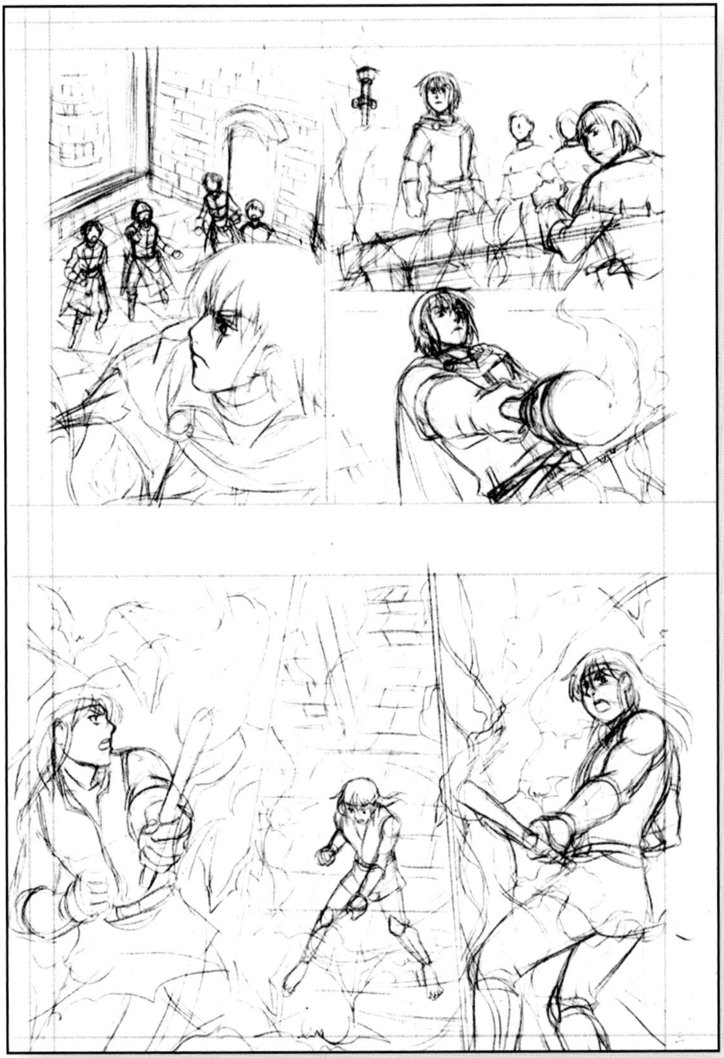

## INKS

When illustrations have been approved by the editor, an artist, sometimes called an "inker," draws over the pencils in ink. This stage allows readers to see the illustration more easily in print.

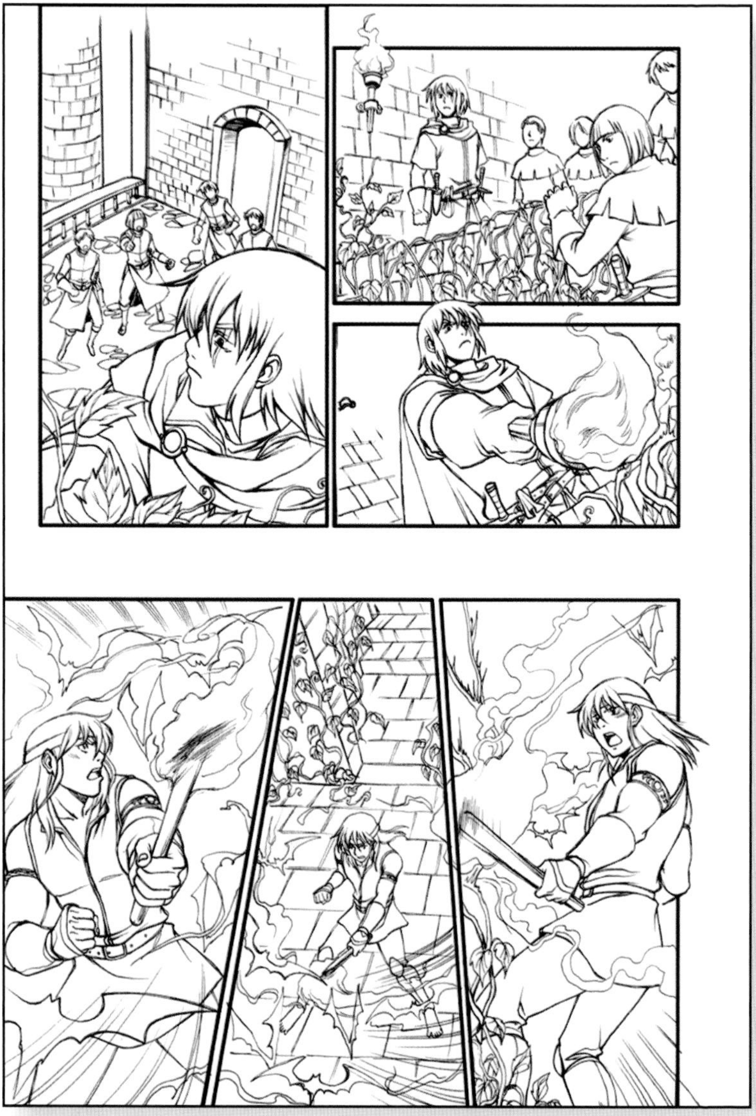

## COLORS

Next, the inks are sent to a "colorist" who adds color to each panel of art.

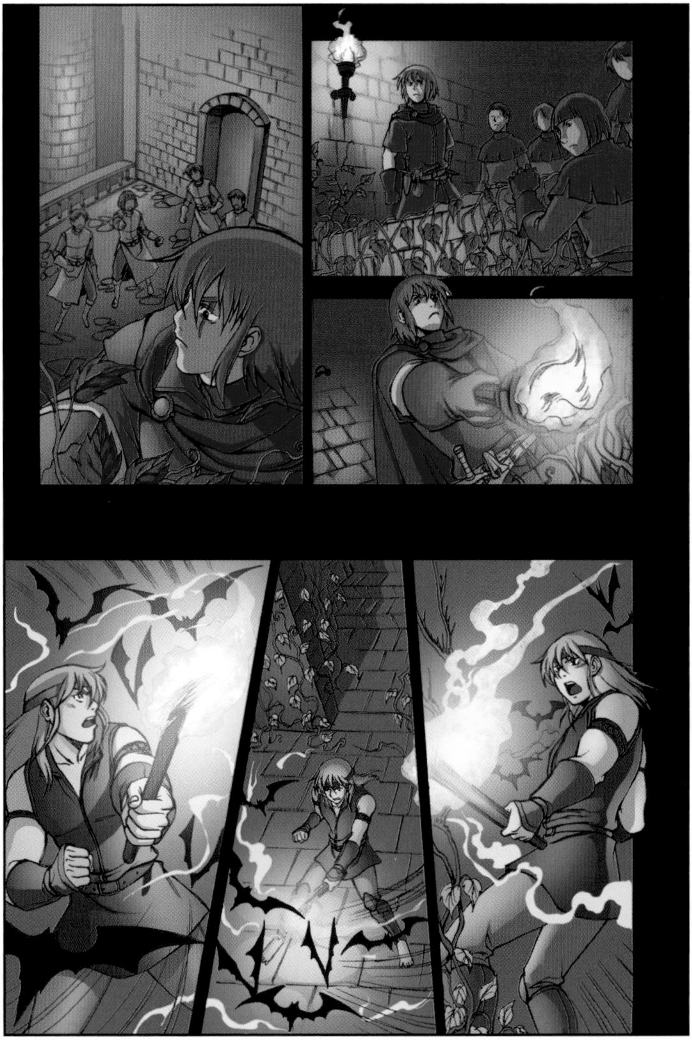

When the art is completed, designers add the final touches, including word balloons and sound effects. Turn to page 12 to see the final version.

# EVERY STORY HAS TWO SIDES...

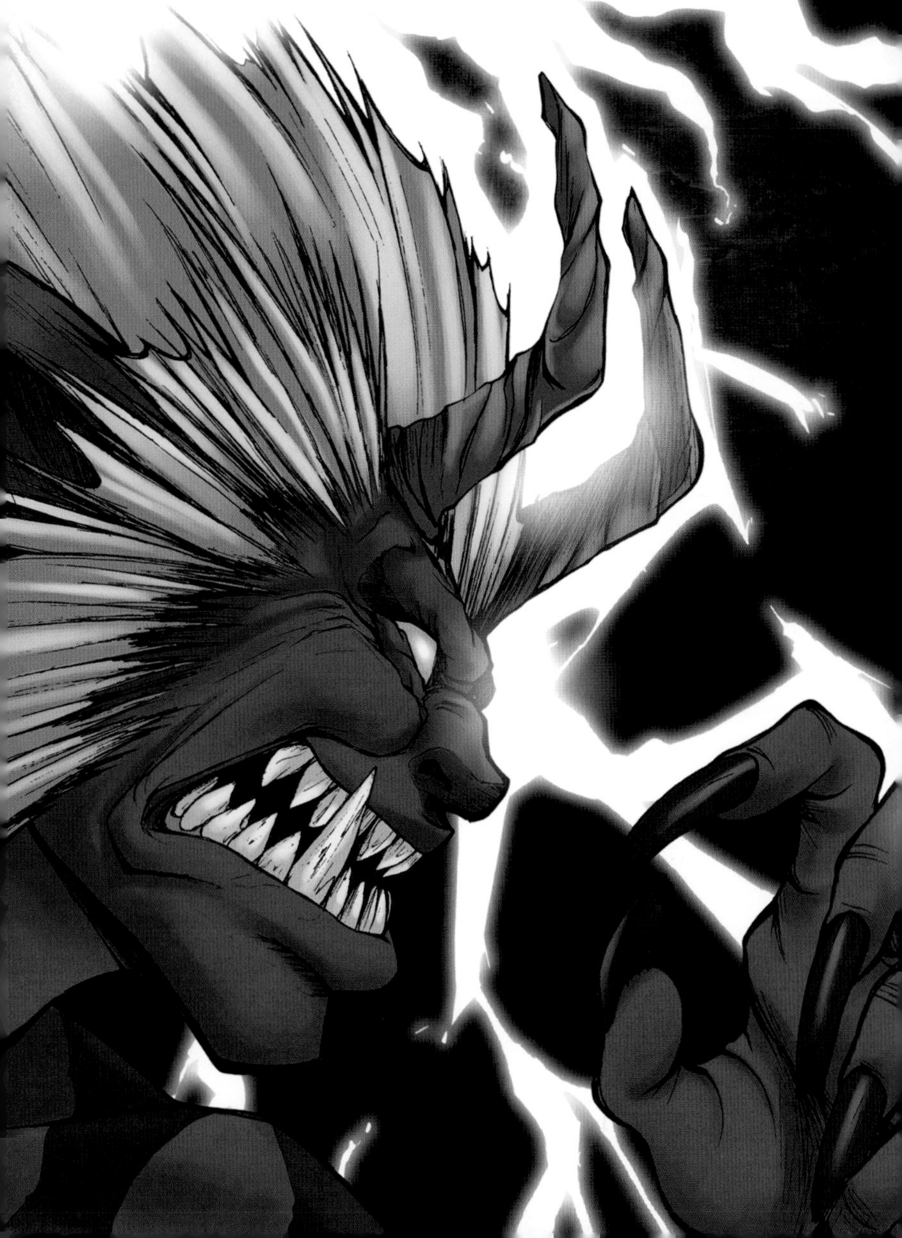

# GOOD VS EVIL

Adventure

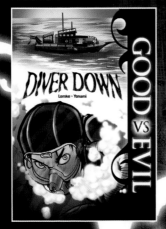

GOOD VS EVIL
DIVER DOWN
Lemke • Yonami

Fantasy

GOOD VS EVIL
DUNGEON OF SEVEN DOOMS
Dahl • Pares

Science Fiction

GOOD VS EVIL
ALIEN SNOW
Dahl • Pares

Horror

THE AWAKENING
Lemke • Medeiros
GOOD VS EVIL

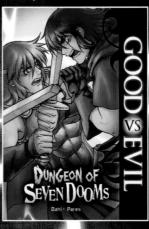

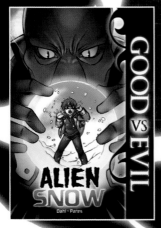

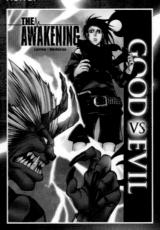

## COLLECT THEM ALL!

GOOD vs EVIL